Barrel Proof

Bourbon Legacy, Volume 4

J. P. Bastin

Published by J. P. Bastin, 2024.

<u>Acknowledgements</u>

Once again, I want to thank my marvelous editor, Natalie. You make my stories shine.

And thank you to Tracie at Dark Waters Covers for yet another wonderful cover design.

Chapter 1

Suz Benton hadn't been able to shake the knot of dread currently residing in her stomach all afternoon. It had nothing to do with the crowd of happy party goers currently milling about, nibbling on the fabulous hors d'oeuvres from the distillery's sparkling new kitchen and sipping on cocktails made from the finest MacInnes bourbon. As an event planner, she could handle that with both hands tied behind her back.

No, it all revolved around one specific member of the family: Matthew MacInnes. Cousin to Colin and Marianne. Marine. Cooper extraordinaire. And in this case, the object of her crush.

"Take the bull by the horns and just talk to him," her bestie Marianne had said when Matt started ghosting.

She scanned over the crowd of guests, a satisfied smile on her face. This new event center at the MacInnes distillery was a party planner's dream venue. But then, she'd been able to feed her suggestions into the facility development through her best friend Marianne MacInnes. Not to mention the three business cards already in her pocket from potential clients.

She circulated the room, checking the buffet tables, chatting with the distillery's guests. Even stopping in the sparkling new kitchen to pop a salmon canape into her mouth before praising the work done by Gray and his staff.

"Have you seen Marianne?" she called back at Gray before leaving the kitchen.

He looked up from the tray of glazed wings he was plating and then shook his head. "Not for over an hour."

"Okay, I need to thank her for loaning me this fabulous dress."

Gray handed the tray off to a waiting server. "You look marvelous as always. Now, out of my kitchen," he added with a shooing motion.

She couldn't resist calling back a very foodie, "Yes, chef," before heading back out into the huge party room.

Suz scanned the room, finally locating Marianne. She and her brother Colin stood with the Kentucky governor chatting, and sipping on what Suz assumed was one of MacInnes Distillery's fine bourbons. Not wanting to interrupt the conversation, she just stepped up behind Marianne before whispering, "Thanks for the dress."

Marianne gave her a wink and whispered back, "Talk later."

After nodding, Suz continued her tour around the room. Surprisingly, everything thus far was running super smooth. Everyone she'd spoken to had high praise for the new facility. No doubt the phone in the booking office would be ringing off the hook come Monday morning as the movers and shakers of Kentucky's gentry jockeyed for prime party slots.

She glanced around the room. There was one more MacInnes she wanted—no, *needed* to talk to this afternoon. Matthew MacInnes.

Marianne's right. Take the bull by the horns. "Just talk to him," her friend had repeatedly said. *Well today's the day.*

"Where are you, Matt?" she said out loud, her words barely above a whisper as she scanned the room. Then she found him, leaning up against one wall, possibly watching the band set up, an empty Glencairn glass in one hand.

Before she lost her nerve, she grabbed him by the free hand, tugging him toward the door leading to the patio. "You. Me. Outside, now. We need to talk."

Once outside, Matt set his glass down on one of the patio tables and then folded his arms across his chest. "Talk about what?"

Letting her head cock to one side, Suz responded, "Seriously? You don't know?"

"So, clue me in, Suzanne." Matt leaned one brawny shoulder against the brick wall.

No thinking about the shoulders. Focus.

"You've been ghosting me. Ever since I had to cancel on that party. That's what."

He shrugged. "I've been busy."

"Too busy for a quick phone call? Hell, even a text message. I know you've got my phone number."

His gaze darted away from her for a split second. And in that moment, his whole demeanor changed.

"Get down!" Matt shouted as he dove toward her, taking them both to the patio floor.

As they hit the concrete, the crack of a rifle shot split the air around them.

# # #

Matt had been waiting for the detective for almost ten minutes when she finally sat down across the table.

"Thank you for being so patient. I got caught up with the forensic techs," Detective Jessica Kent flipped open her ever present notebook.

"Did they find anything?"

She nodded. "The bullet. You already know it did a through and through on your new four by four post."

"I'm sure Colin's gonna have me fixing that on Monday." Matt elbowed his cousin in the ribs.

"It lodged in that tree over there." Jess pointed before adding, "The angles jibe with where you say you saw the lens flare. By the way, that was a damned lucky catch."

"Not when you've spent combat time."

"You know I have to ask this." Colin leaned forward in his chair. "Is this connected to everything else that's been happening around here?"

Matt had been trying not to imagine that someone would deliberately try to shoot any of the MacInnes extended family. "I could've been an accident, right? Some jerk of a hunter not watching beyond his target?"

"Always a possibility. But guys, I'll tell you this, just between us. Unless I get rock solid proof otherwise, I'm going on the assumption that anything out of the ordinary here is connected."

Once Jess had left the table, Colin asked, "You okay?"

"My palm hurts like hell from the concrete and I'm pretty sure when I take my pants off, I'll see both of my knees are scraped."

Colin gave him one of those *you goofball* looks. "You know what I mean." Matt's cousin tapped him on the forehead. "Up here?"

"Right now, yeah. A week, a month. Heck, six months or even a year from now, who the hell knows, Colin? You've dealt with PTSD. You know how it is."

"And just like you've been there for me, I'm here for you. Twenty-four seven, three-sixty-five."

"And don't think I don't appreciate that." Matt smacked his cousin on the back. "I should, umm, go check on Suz. I knocked her down kinda rough. I want to make sure she's okay."

"Good idea."

As Matt walked back inside the party room, he could swear his cousin was snickering.

The guests had all departed, leaving just the clean-up crew and Gray's kitchen staff. No loud banter and teasing tonight. Everyone all but tiptoed around. Matt knew for certain that Suz had been shaken to her core. When they'd hit the deck, she'd trembled like a leaf in a tornado.

As the seconds ticked by after the shot rang out, he'd whispered to her to stay down. Matt crept over to one of the tables before peeking over it at where he'd seen the lens flare. Nothing. Zip. Nada. After scanning all around the area, he'd still seen nothing. Only then did he creep back to where Suz still lay on the concrete floor.

He'd wanted to hug her close, reassuring her that the threat was gone. Instead, he'd carefully helped her stay low as they slipped back inside. Matt handed Suz off to Marianne as he went in search of Colin.

Now that all the excitement of the party had settled down, all Matt wanted to do was to ensure Suz was okay and that she got home safely before finally heading homeward himself. He couldn't help being over protective where Marianne's best friend was concerned. He'd had a serious crush on her since the day they'd met years ago.

Maybe now he should do something about that.

He located Suz, sitting with Marianne at a small table, a glass in front of each of them. His cousin's looked like it had barely been touched. But the one Suz toyed with was nearly empty.

As he walked to the table, both women looked up, Marianne with a knowing smile.

"Matt, would you make sure Suz gets home? I poured a double so I don't want her driving."

"Sure thing." He nodded.

She stood up from her chair. "Good. I'll go see if there's anything I can do to help the clean-up crew." Marianne hugged her friend. "Let Matt get you home. Take a good, steamy shower, put your PJ's on, and then curl up with a good book. Something with a hot, sexy hero."

Suz was looking right at him when she flushed at the mention of a sexy hero. *Maybe Marianne is right. Maybe Suz is interested.*

When his cousin had walked away, Matt took the chair she'd vacated. "Did you get hurt when I shoved you down?"

She shook her head. "Nothing serious. But I'm not sure I can say the same about Marianne's dress." Suz flipped the loose end of one of the spaghetti straps that had been pulled from its attachment point. "Not to mention the side seam now stops north of my hips."

A mental image formed in his head—one long slim thigh and the curve of her sweet backside, exposed for his own enjoyment. He tried, only half successfully, to tamp that thought back into the recesses of his imagination before the effects became obvious. He also did his best not to look down on her thighs. So hard to do...

"Here." He shrugged out of his sport coat. "It's long enough to at least keep you mostly covered."

"Thanks," she muttered as she stood, letting him help her slide her arms into the coat. "But really, I'm okay to drive."

"Not legally. It looks like half of the Frankfort PD is out there. Not to mention two or three county mounties and even a couple of staties that came with Detective Kent." Matt scooped up her tiny purse before offering her his arm. "Nope. I'm afraid you're stuck with an escort home."

# # #

"You know it helps to talk about it."

The street lights had begun to come on and cast long shadows in Matt's car. "What's there to talk about?"

He glanced over at her while idling the classic VW Bug at a stop light. "In case you've forgotten, we were shot at this afternoon."

"It was an accident. Had to be." Suz sat stock still, staring straight out the windshield.

Matt muttered something intelligible as he shifted gears and drove.

"What did you say?" She turned to him and he threw her a quick glance.

"I said, accident my ass."

"You really think someone shot at us on purpose?"

"Yes. As do Colin and Detective Kent." He turned down her street.

The idea that someone would actually shoot at people—people who were doing nothing more than going about their business, a threat to no one... Just unfathomable. It was hard enough for her to imagine shooting a person who seeks to do harm. She shuddered in her seat.

"You? Me? Who was the target?" Maybe if she had more details to hang her hat on, it would be easier to comprehend.

"Who knows? Maybe neither of us. Maybe the only thing that put us in the crosshairs was our presence at the party this afternoon." He turned from the street into the townhouse complex. "Which one is yours?"

"Down at the end. The one with the fall wreath on the door."

Matt pulled in at the curb, into the spot where her SUV usually sat. He turned off the engine before turning to her. "Want me to go inside first?"

She shook her head. "No, I'm okay. Though how am I going to get my car back?"

"I can pick you up in the morning. Got any place you need to be at a specific time tomorrow?"

Suz mentally flipped through her calendar. "I don't think so but let me check my phone." She fished it out of her purse before tapping the screen to life and scrolled through her electronic calendar. "Nope, Nothing until a phone call middle of the afternoon with a potential client."

"Great. I'll come pick you up about ten-thirty."

"Sounds like a plan." She opened the door and then unbuckled her seatbelt. "See you in the morning."

# # #

Once she was safely behind the locked front door, Suz flicked the porch light off and back on a couple of times to let Matt know she was inside and okay. Then and only then did she lean back against the door, before sliding down until her butt reached the floor.

The shakes started with her hands, making her drop her keys and letting them clatter onto the entryway tiles. As the shakes spread throughout her body, her eyes filled with moisture, causing fearful tears to run down both cheeks. Her jaw quivered as the reality of the evening finally sank in. *S-S-Someone sh-sh-shot at me. At me and Matt.*

His headlights had been long gone by the time she regained control and shuffled off in search of a tissue. Suz sniffled and blew her nose after wiping away the last of the tears. *This must be what Matt meant when he asked if I was okay.* Maybe she should take Marianne's advice.

Ten minutes later, she was shoulder-deep in lavender-scented bubbles, with the latest motorcycle romance novel audiobook playing on her tablet. Yet somehow, tonight, the hot Harley-riding dude couldn't hold her attention. Matthew MacInnes kept creeping into her imagination. Broad shoulders and biceps to die for, being a cooper for the family distillery had done his physique good. Not to mention the time he'd spent in Uncle Sam's Marine Corps.

No wonder he had been calm and cool once the shot had rung out. She figured this wasn't the first time he'd been a shooting target. Heck, as part of the MacInnes family, he'd grown up around firearms.

I, on the other hand. . .

Suz knew exactly what she was: the quintessential city girl. Born and raised in Louisville, her father having climbed the academic ladder from professor to dean of the mathematics department at U of L with her homemaker mother by his side. That's where Suz had begun her party planning training, at the knee of a woman who could hostess rings around Martha Stewart.

Summer afternoons were spent with her friends in the backyard pool or at the mall. School years were filled with gymnastic meets and cheer squad. Her grades came easy and dates were frequent. The sweet sixteen party her mom had planned had been nothing less than epic.

Then, out of the blue, during her junior year of college, the great wheel of chance had spun Marianne MacInnes into Suz's life. First as a roommate, then as a friend, confidante, and co-conspirator. Then, finally, as door-opener to all things foreign to Suz's urban upbringing.

Were she and Matt too different? Nope, she refused to consider it just because she liked bubble baths, white wine, and rom-com movies on Hallmark. She doubted he'd ever tasted a good German gewurztraminer or watched anything on the Hallmark channel. Now the image of him immersed in a tub of bubbles, with her of course ... that was a completely different thing.

A shudder raced through her body, settling between her thighs. Her fingers trailed along the same path, over her breasts, stopping to circle her pebbled nipples before sliding over her skin to the smooth folds hiding her clit. She leaned her head back against the waterproof pillow, letting the sensations build. Stroking and circling the taut bundle of sensitive flesh, she finally gave herself over to yet another of her Matt MacInnes fueled climaxes.

# # #

The sky has just started to streak with the Sunday morning sunrise as Sheriff Whitaker pulled into the parking lot. Most of the men on night shift would be typing up reports of any actions over the previous eight hours or sitting in some drive-through line getting one last cup of coffee for the drive home. His day shift crew were likely still at home filling go-cups before kissing wives and girlfriends good-bye before starting the drive to the station house.

Once in his parking spot right by the back entrance—rank did have its privileges—he got out to open the trunk. As he lifted the silvery gun case out, Whitaker ran the story through his mind one final time. Any of the deputies he might run into would accept the tale of taking a rifle to the department's range to sight in a new scope before the upcoming start of deer season. Once inside, getting into the evidence room and then to the gun locker would be a piece of cake.

He'd heard the radio traffic on his way back from the woods yesterday. He'd made sure to contact his watch commander during the aftermath, and then made a call to the chief of police. Later today, he planned to call that detective working the problems at MacInnes as she chased her tail. Yup, nothing now but a nice relaxing Sunday afternoon.

# # #

Ten-twenty-five, and Matt pulled the VW into the parking spot allotted to the townhouse resident for the second time in less than a day. During the whole drive over to her place, he'd mentally debated asking her to join him for a meal. *Brunch,* he'd corrected himself. Women like her set a great store in using fancy names. He'd vacillated, before finally settling on the nothing ventured, nothing gained approach.

He'd just opened the door to get out when Suz closed her front door and headed his direction. Matt waved. "Morning, sunshine."

She tossed her wallet and keys onto the dash. "Coffee, please. I overslept," she replied as she buckled her seatbelt.

"Yes, Ma'am."

A quick and silent five-minute drive later, he was reaching out the car window for two large coffees from Mickey D's drive-thru. "Here." He handed her one of the cups before circling

the building and pulled into one of the empty parking spaces without shutting the engine. He popped the lid off his, blew across the dark steamy surface, then took a tentative sip. And another. And then yet another.

"I think I'm human now." Suz leaned back in the seat. "Mostly anyway. I slept like hell last night."

"Why?" Matt had a feeling he knew the reason. Yet, there was a part of him that wanted to see if she would actually admit the why.

"I, umm, I don't know. couldn't stay asleep. I'd wake up every hour or so and then pitch and toss for a while, trying to get back to sleep. One of those things, I guess." She paused for another couple of sips from her coffee. "We all have the occasional restless night."

"Oh, yeah. Been there many times." He stifled a laugh. *If that's how she wants to spin it.*

Matt knew exactly why she hadn't slept well, whether she wanted to admit it to him ... or herself. Yesterday still had her rattled. He'd bet the farm on it.

He decided to let her stew in her thoughts during the drive to the distillery. *Unless she starts up a conversation.* But as he expected, the rest of the drive was as silent as the first.

Once he turned off the state highway onto MacInnes grounds, he took the first cut off to the new event center. He had to give Uncle James and Colin credit; the project had turned out to be damn near perfect. But then they'd gotten input not only from the architect and contractor, but also from Gray for the kitchen facilities and Suz for making the space event friendly. The glowing write up in the papers everyone had been expecting was now overshadowed by stories of the shooting.

There, up near the back entrance to the new facility, sat Suz's SUV all by itself. He pulled the VW up beside it. "Here you are."

As she scooped her purse up off the floor, Matt added, "Listen, when all hell broke loose yesterday, you wanted to talk about how I've been avoiding you."

Suz took her hand off the door handle before turning to face him. "And?"

"It wasn't on purpose." She rolled her eyes. "Okay, not completely. A little bit, I admit."

"So, what do you intend to do about that?"

"First, apologize. I'm sorry. I meant to say so sooner, but one thing led to another, and it just snowballed. Seriously, I am sorry."

She drew in a deep breath then blew it out. "Apology accepted." Suz reach for the door handle again, but then stopped and turned back toward him. "Now what?"

Put your cards on the table. "If you're still open to the idea, I'd like for us to go out next weekend. Whatever day you're free."

He could swear he saw the beginnings of a smile light up her face.

"I've got a company party in Louisville Friday evening. But how about Saturday?"

"That's perfect. How about I call you the middle of the week? We'll firm up plans then." *Damn, do I have to sound so frikken formal?*

Her smile widened. "Sounds like a winner. Tuesday or Wednesday. Any time after six, if that's okay."

He nodded. "Yeah. I've got some presentation barrels to build this week. Any preferences?"

"Surprise me." Without warning, she leaned over and gave him a quick kiss before opening the passenger door. "I'm gonna want more of those," she declared before pushing the door open and jumping out, closing it behind her.

He watched, more than a bit gobsmacked, as she unlocked the SUV and got into the driver's seat. *Man, oh, man, this is going to be fun.*

Chapter 2

Suz had spent the rest of the day running the errands she'd put off to attend the party at MacInnes' new event center. Now everything she'd procured and purchased for the coming week's events had been tucked away in the storage room at her downtown office. The single bag from the grocery had already been put away in her kitchen.

Naked with her robe tossed over one shoulder, she headed to the bathroom for a well-deserved soak in a hot bubble bath. As the tub filled, Suz added a generous amount of lavender oil to the bubble mix. After the past twenty-four hours, she needed the relaxation.

Her fingers and toes were all crinkled up when she finally toweled off. She'd tried her best to concentrate on the spy thriller novel she'd been reading. Instead of cheering the hero on toward finding the bomb in the US Capitol building, her mind kept wandering to a certain broad- shouldered cooper.

She'd been crushing on Matthew MacInnes for nearly a decade, ever since she and Marianne had been college roommates their sophomore year. Marianne had invited Suz to the MacInnes family's Thanksgiving when Suz had let slip her parents were heading to Colorado, both for skiing and visiting her older brother at the Air Force Academy.

"No one should spend Thanksgiving alone if they don't have to. And you don't have to. Come home with me," Marianne had insisted.

Thus had begun her entry into the MacInnes clan. Matt had been home for the holidays before starting his second deployment to what he and Colin both called the sandbox—and following her visit, he'd starred in innumerable fantasies during the rest of her college years. She still carried an image in her head of how he'd looked in that dress blues uniform.

Now ... she'd kissed him. *Kinda*. It had been barely more than a brotherly peck, but she'd landed it right on his lips and that had set her pulse racing. She reached up to touch her lips, half expecting to find them still tingling.

She hung up her towel to dry before heading back into her bedroom. After pulling on fresh panties and her sleep shirt, Suz made one final trip through the house, checking door locks and turning off lights. Then, she grabbed a glass of water in the kitchen before heading off to bed.

# # #

The sound of the shot split the air around them.

"Get down!" Matt shouted, knocking her on the concrete.

Awakened with a start, Suz sat bolt upright in bed, heart pounding in her chest as she gasped for air. When her mind cleared of the nightmare, she reached over for the water glass. Her hand shook so much, she sloshed water onto her sleepshirt. She took one sip, then a second. Finally, a third before she managed to pull in a deep and ragged breath.

She shuddered so uncontrollably that it took both hands to put the glass back on her nightstand. Knowing what had caused the horrible dream wasn't making it any easier to recover. Reliving the horrifying event from yesterday had her once again shaking like a leaf in a windstorm.

It would be futile to try and go right back to her slumber, so she flicked on the bedside lamp. "Three forty," she said out loud to the empty room. "I'll be lucky if I get back to sleep."

When she trusted her quivering legs enough, Suz slid out of bed and shuffled over to the small bookcase on the other side of the room. She trailed a finger over the spines, searching for something to distract her from the remnants of the dream. Something she didn't have to think about too hard. *Yeah, that rom-com I bought last summer but never got around to reading.*

She tugged the novel loose from the others before heading back to bed.

# # #

The fall sunrise was just a rosy glow in the eastern sky as Sheriff Dave Whitaker pulled into his parking spot. He'd debated whether he should arrive early or late for what he had to do this morning—finally settling on early. The day watch hadn't begun to arrive yet, and the night crew were likely typing up reports, while slugging down coffee to stay awake.

Fortunately, he knew where each and every surveillance camera was located. Better still, where the blind and nearly blind spots were. And he'd made sure his car sat at the very edge of visibility.

Whitaker opened the back seat door on the passenger's side. He reached in and pulled the soft-side gun case out, using the car to block the camera's view. Then, he made a show of retrieving his laptop case before smacking the door closed and using the key fob to lock the vehicle.

Instead of heading right to his office, the sheriff headed to the evidence room. The young deputy overseeing the secure area greeted him with a smile and wave.

"Morning, boss."

"Morning, Boone."

"Say, boss, you got time to watch the cage for just a few minutes? I need to run down and get the printout of what the courthouse needs today."

"Sure thing." The deputy was nothing if not predictable. Every morning, like clockwork, the bailiff sent over a list of evidence needed for whatever trial appeared on that day's docket. A uniformed officer would be over soon to sign out the items.

Boone hit the electronic lock granting the sheriff entry. Once the deputy left, Whitaker used the key to open the weapons locker. He then opened the gun case he'd carried in and removed the .308 caliber rifle using the clean handkerchief he'd left wrapped around the stock. Without touching anything else, he returned the gun to the numbered slot he'd taken it from on Friday.

That rifle had been confiscated when a young punk had held up a quick mart with a nine-millimeter automatic. Since the long gun hadn't been used in the crime, but had simply been found in the truck at impound, it had been logged in as property until they could find out if it was a stolen firearm—and no official ballistics had been performed.

With the door lock clicked back into place, the sheriff wiped the fastener down. It paid to know about every weapon in the evidence locker.

# # #

Matt elbowed the blackberry briar out of the way as he led his cousin Colin through the woods. The investigators had already combed the area where the shooter had hidden.

"Tell me again why we're out here? Jess's team has been all over the spot and found nothing but some flattened grass."

"I want to see for myself. Don't you?" Matt slowed his pace before finally stopping.

Colin walked up beside him. "Well, yeah. But I doubt we're gonna find anything new."

"You never know." Bending down, Matt raked his fingers through the sparse grass. "I saw a lens flare, so we know the shooter was using a scoped rifle."

"Thank heaven you did. You or Suz could've been injured," Colin took a deep breath before continuing, "or worse."

"That thought has crossed my mind. Repeatedly I might add." Matt stood up. "Looks like the shooter was prone, about six feet give or take a bit. Gotta assume it's a man."

Colin nodded. "You only heard one shot, right?"

"Yup. I'm guessing that once he realized the shot missed whichever of us was the actual target, he hightailed it out of here, without taking the risk of a second try."

Colin looked around. "That's what I'd do. But which way?"

"I'd want my car as close as possible. Now if I remember right, there's really only two ways to drive into these woods." Matt pointed back in the direction he and Colin had walked. "The old farm road we used." Colin nodded as Matt turned around. "And the old Simpson place over there."

"No one's lived there since we were kids. Remember how old man Simpson use to chase us off the property if we cut through there?"

"Peppered us with rock salt from that old twenty-gauge one time." Matt rubbed one hand over his ass, remembering the pain. "You ever park out there while back in high school?"

"I can neither confirm nor deny any such lascivious activities."

Matt laughed. "Yeah, me neither." He took a couple of steps in that direction before he knelt. "Bingo." He pointed into the weeds. "Heading right towards the Simpson house."

They walked parallel to the shooter's trail to keep from destroying the evidence of the escape route, finally arriving at the abandoned house. "I was out here hunting mushrooms a couple of years ago. Ducked under what was left of the porch to get out of the rain for a bit."

"Bet last winter's snow took it down," Colin added as they circled around to the front of the old house.

"Tells me our shooter is a local. Likely no one else would know about this place." Matt walked over to where the ancient mailbox clung to its post by a single nail. "Look here, tire marks in the weeds."

"Get some pictures with your phone."

"No shit, Sherlock," Matt rolled his eyes at his cousin. "Look, he did a three-point turn around and then headed back to the main road."

Pulling his phone from one of his shirt pockets, he captured the trail of tire marks.

"We'll do the same with the path he used from here to the place he chose for the shot."

"You gonna let Detective Kent know what we found?" Matt was beginning to think they needed to keep the facts confined to a really tight circle. They'd recently had one distillery employee wreak havoc. The fewer the people who knew what had transpired, the better he'd feel.

"I will. I'll talk to her tomorrow, ask her to meet me for coffee or something away from the distillery."

"Sounds like you and I are on the same page." Matt shoved his phone into the back pocket of his jeans.

Colin nodded. "Roger that. Let's head back."

# # #

Sheriff Whitaker had just left Sylvie Prather's tiny house over in the old part of town. He'd stop by every now and then, when he had an urge for something different. Something his wife couldn't—no, wouldn't—provide.

He'd just gotten back into his beat up, old sedan, the one he kept stashed away for times like this, when his cell phone rang. "Damn," he muttered under his breath, knowing exactly who would be on the other end of the call.

"Yes, Ma'am." Whitaker braced himself for the dressing down he knew was coming.

"You incompetent imbecile."

"I can explain, Judge."

"Spare me your excuses, Whitaker. Not only did you miss the shot, but that wasn't even the MacInnes bitch."

No way. "That's impossible. I saw the red dress myself, clear as day, through the scope."

Several silent seconds ticked by before Judge Madeline Barnes continued. "If you would watch the local news, Sheriff," her words dripped with a tone of superiority Whitaker had heard hundreds of times in the judge's courtroom, "you'd have heard you shot at Marianne MacInnes's best friend, Suzanne something-or-other."

Before he could get a word in edgewise, Judge Barnes went on, "If you'd been successful, I could forgive your sloppy marksmanship."

Whitaker's temper burst into flames. "Sloppy? Sloppy. I'll have you know that bullet went right where I wanted it. How in the hell that dude knew the shot was coming, I'll never know."

"That's because he's a combat veteran, a Marine, you fool. Told the news reporter he saw the lens flare."

A Marine. That made Whitaker feel a little better. "I'll get that MacInnes lady next time, Judge."

"No, you won't because there will be no next time. You botched this—now the whole damn clan is going to be extremely careful. No, I have something better in mind for those thieving MacInneses."

With that, the call went dead.

Whitaker knew better than to try and call Judge Barnes back. The phone she'd used to make the call would already be turned off and secured. He'd taught her that himself years ago.

He'd have to do something to get back into her good graces. Even though she'd retired years ago and moved back into the family home south of Richmond, Judge Madeline Barnes still had undeniable influence here in Franklin County. She could kill any hope he might have of a third term with a single statement of non-confidence.

He thought for a moment before settling on an idea. That Marine, the one who'd ruined the shot—all he to do was find out who the man was and take him out.

Child's play. Sheriff Whitaker started the car before pulling away from the curb. He'd present the Judge with a *fait accompli. Then we'll see who gets called incompetent.*

# # #

"This was the Monday-est Wednesday I've had in months." Suz butt-bumped her apartment door closed as she juggled her purse, computer case, and two bags from a stop at the grocery on the way home. "'Course it would've helped if I'd slept good last night."

"Oh?" Marianne's voice had a tell-me-more tone.

"Stop it." Suz shrugged the purse off her shoulder, followed by the computer case, both landing on the couch. "I just kept waking up and then having trouble getting back to sleep." No way was she going to tell even her best friend about the dreams. "Guess it was that huge cup of coffee on the way home from my client meeting."

"Late night coffee never used to bother you."

"Well, umm," Suz struggled for an excuse, anything other than mentioning another nightmare. "We aren't twenty-year-old college students anymore. You and I are both staring thirty in the face, ya know." She put the bags on the kitchen counter.

"Yeah, yeah. Bite me." Marianne went silent and then giggled. "Stop it, Gray. I'm on the phone."

A twinge of envy flashed through Suz. It was hard enough to keep her thoughts off Matt, without knowing her friend on the other end of this call had her own hunk flirting with her at this very moment.

"Maybe I should let you go?"

Another giggle from her friend was followed by a very masculine, "Delicious."

"Maybe you'd better. Seems like someone wants attention." Marianne paused then added, "And maybe dinner."

Suz put the package of cold cuts and cheese into the refrigerator. "Talk to you tomorrow."

After the rest of her grocery haul had been put away, she chose one of the frozen dinners and then popped the plastic tray into her microwave. As her dinner heated, Suz got her planner from the computer bag and flipped it open to the next day's page.

By the time eleven o'clock rolled around, she'd been fighting sleep for more than an hour as she finished the necessary prep for her Thursday. Suz shoved her laptop and planner back into the computer bag before turning off the lights and heading for the shower.

# # #

The sound of the shot split the air around them.

"Get down!" Matt shouted, knocking her onto the concrete.

"What was that?" Suz ignored the jolt of pain from both knees as they scraped over the ground.

"A rifle shot," Matt whispered against her ear.

Another shot cracked through the air. "It's coming from the woods."

She shuddered as fear took a frosty hold around her chest. "But ... but why is someone shooting at us?"

"No clue, just stay the hell down. And keep quiet." Matt inched over and flipped one of the tables onto its side. "Stay behind this."

Fear knotted in her chest. Chips of brick burst into the air as yet another shot hit the side of the building behind them. Suz bit her lip in an effort to keep from screaming.

A third shot thudded into the table and then a fourth sent splinters flying in all directions as it took a chunk out of the wood. "Matt, please, do something."

"I'm not armed, darlin.'" Matt started to peer over the table when yet another shot whizzed past, the bullet embedding itself in one of the cedar support posts.

"My phone is in my purse. In Marianne's office. You have yours?"

He shook his head. "Back up in the cooperage."

Suz jumped when the next shot ricocheted off the concrete before shattering one of the building's windows. "We gotta get out of here!"

"Trust me, I know." Another shot had both of them diving to the floor. "Can we get inside?"

"I...I don't know."

"Okay, stay down. I'm gonna check."

Suz squeezed his hand. "Be careful."

Matt did a tuck 'n roll to table behind them. Once under it, he turned and flashed her a thumbs up. She watched as he left the protection of the table for the final dash to the door.

Just as his hand reach out for the door, one more shot split the silence.

Suz screamed as she sat bolt upright in bed.

# # #

"Q, that's ten," Marianne declared, placing a tile on the board. "U, E, using your S, my dear Suz. And T. That makes fourteen." She wrote on the score pad. "Oh, double word, that makes twenty-eight. And poof, back in the lead."

Jenni gave her a high five. "That rocks. I've never been able to use a Q when I get it."

"Hey, whose side are you on?" Suz fought unsuccessfully to stifle a yawn. "This is every woman for herself."

Marianne gave her friend a questioning side glance, as if she suspected the truth. "Still not sleeping well?"

"Bet she's all hot and bothered, having wild, erotic dreams featuring our resident cooper," Jenni chimed in.

"So, you're finally going out with Matt?" Marianne looked up from the scoresheet.

"What if I am?"

"Nothin'. It's about time is all." Marianne's eyes rolled. "You two have been mooning over one another forever."

"She's right, ya know." Jennie moved her tiles around as she spoke. "You were hot for him when Col and I were dating the first time."

"Don't go ordering bouquets just yet. It's only one date. Probably nothing more than burgers and a movie." Suz leaned back into the couch cushions.

"Okay, if we can't talk about you jonesing for my cousin," Marianne grabbed up a chip and scooped up some of the salsa, crunched it in her mouth and swallowed, "let's talk about the other elephant in the room. You, my friend, haven't been sleeping well since the shooting happened. Let me take a wild guess here. Nightmares?"

Suz responded with a tiny nod. Pointing at both of her friends, she added, "This doesn't leave this room. Got it?"

"Colin had one last week," Jenni replied. "First time it happened, scared the bejeebers outta me. He bolted up out of bed in a cold sweat, shaking like he was chilling with a fever

"That's it exactly. I've had nightmares before. Like after watching some scary movie." Suz rubbed her arms against the non-existent cold. "But those were always one or two and done. Last night," she had to swallow hard before going on, "the shots kept coming. And there was no one around to help us."

"Us? Matt, too?"

"So far, yeah. It's all been variations on the real shooting."

Marianne rose from the chair she'd taken when they started the game, moving over to sit beside her friend and hug her. "You wake up and need someone to talk to, call me. Anytime."

"Me, too." Jenni plunked down on Suz's other side.

"Thanks, you two. I'm not sleeping well but they aren't bad nightmares." *Yet.* "I promise. I'll call if I need you."

They played another round. When her turn came again, Jenni held her tile before putting it onto the board. "I just thought of something." Using the wooden tile as a pointer, she directed it at Suz, "What if..." She put the tile down. "What if Matt was the target, not you? I mean we don't actually know, do we?"

"Oh, shit." Suz gasped. "We haven't really talked about that. What if he's in danger? I've got to call him. Tonight."

Both Marianne and Jenni nodded.

"Or you." Suz looked over at Marianne. "Remember, I was wearing one of your dresses. What if the shooter thought it was you in the crosshairs?"

Marianne's eyes went wide and her jaw dropped. "No," she shook her head. "No, can't be. That was Oscar. And he died in that car crash."

"Colin insists that Oscar was just a puppet. There's a brain behind this whole thing." Jenni shook her head. "I have a feeling that until that person is caught, none of us are safe."

Chapter 3

Jessica Kent hurried down the hall, heading to the stairwell. She'd been summoned to the mayor's office. His honor wanted answers, the sooner the better. Trouble was, she didn't have any. Facts? Those she had plenty of, but answers? None, zero, zip.

"Detective Kent. Jess. Wait up!" shouted a voice from behind her.

Jess glanced back over her shoulder. Terri, one of the ballistics techs, ran down the hall, waving a manilla file folder. "I've got your ballistics report."

"Put a hustle on it. And please tell me you've got a match. I'm heading downtown to brief the mayor. I need something concrete to tell him."

Terri shook her head. "'Fraid not. It was a run of the mill three-oh-eight, hundred and fifty-eight grain bullet. A standard hunting round. No match in the system. Sorry, Jess. I can't even tell you for certain what brand of ammo it's from. My gut says it's a Winchester round, but ..." she shrugged her shoulders before handing Jess the folder.

"Damn. I was afraid of that.' Jess smacked the folder against the wall. She blew out a frustrated breath. "Thanks anyway, Terri. I know you put a rush on this for me."

"No problem. Tell the mayor, umm, yeah, tell him the tests were inconclusive. Or that the database is down. That'll buy you at least a couple of days. You could have something concrete by then."

Jess shrugged. The suggestions were too close to lying. No way was she going to head down that road. Nope, the mayor deserved the truth. No matter what.

She waved at Terri before heading down the stairs and then out to the parking lot. She pulled in a deep breath of the crisp autumn air. Some days, it was totally worth parking on the back row.

Her phone buzzed as she pulled out onto the street. She gave the screen a tap. "Well, if it isn't my favorite medical examiner."

"I'd better be since you woke up in my bed this morning."

Jess and Franklin County's M.E. Dr. James Graham had been enjoying a friend with benefits relationship for over two years. Lately though, things had been tipping over into relationship land, with her spending most nights at his condo.

"There is that." Jess laughed. "How's your day going?"

"Coroner's office sent an unidentified D.B. early this morning. I'm gonna have to beg off our lunch date. This is going to take a while."

"I heard about that." She flicked on her turn signal. Jim had used the short-cut, abbreviation for dead body. "Female, forty-ish. Found out on Highway Sixty, south of the shopping center?"

"That's her. One of the night shift sheriff deputies found her and called it in. No car, no I.D."

"Want me to bring you something?"

"If you've got time."

The stoplight changed and Jess made the turn onto Third Street toward city hall. "I'm heading to the mayor's office. He wants a face-to-face update on this MacInnes thing. I'll pick you up lunch once I get done there."

"That'd be great. You making any progress on that?"

Even though she knew he couldn't see her, Jess shook her head. "I wish. I got nothing but vandalism, contamination, explosions, and not one, but two, dead bodies. Now, some wacko with a rifle and not a ballistics match to be found."

"Not good."

"So very not good. I may need to be cheered up this evening. You up for it, big guy?"

Jim's deep baritone chuckle caressed her ears. "Always."

# # #

"Where are you taking me?"

"I told you casual and delicious, didn't I?"

Suz looked out the window as they crossed the river. "Yes, you did."

Matt pulled his classic VW Bug into a parking spot. "I thought you might like a brat and a beer at Sig's."

She grinned. "I haven't been to the Taproom in ages. Oh. I already know what I want."

Once he'd set the parking brake, he asked, "What's that?"

"A big beer brat with sauerkraut. And one of their draft beers."

"Oh, good," Matt looked relieved. "I know I told you casual, but I was a bit nervous about the choice. I mean. You go to all those swanky parties you help plan. Champagne and caviar. First class all the way."

Suz belted out a laugh. "I may go to dozens of fancy parties, but there's nothing like simple and delicious food along with a hot date."

The short walk to the restaurant, Suz told him about a near disaster she'd had last week while working with a bridezilla who kept insisting she wanted the doves dyed blue. "She just couldn't get it through her head that there are regulations preventing that."

He shook his head. "I don't know how you keep your cool dealing with folks like that. I figure it must happen a lot with all of those monied, social mavens."

"Actually, those old money ones are the easiest to please. It's the," she paused to find the right word, "the *nouveau riche* that tend to be more inflexible."

"One of the reasons I leave the stuff out in front of the public to Colin and Marianne. I can smile and wave with the best of them."

Once at the restaurant, Matt asked the hostess to seat them out on the patio. The evening crowd has just begun to arrive, enabling them to be seated immediately. Their server arrived right on the heels of the hostess's departure and quickly took their orders.

Conversation came easy between them. When she mentioned a dilemma of how to display a collection of antique crystal and keep with the western theme of the party, Matt offered to lend a few bourbon barrels.

"That would be fabulous. Thanks." She reached across the table to give his hand a squeeze, sending a prickle through her skin.

Their food and drinks arrived sparking a light-hearted debate on whether or not to mustard a brat when you have sauerkraut as a side. Matt was solidly in the no mustard camp, whereas Suz defended her mustard stance.

"The grainier the better," she declared.

They were almost finished with their meal as the band started setting up.

"These guys are good." She dabbed at her lips to get off the last of the mustard. "I heard them the last time I was here back in the spring."

"Not many our age like jazz." Matt pushed his plate to the side.

"I blame my dad. He's got a huge collection of jazz along with big band stuff." She smiled at the memory her mind conjured up. "I remember one night. I think I was about seven. I went downstairs to get a glass of water.

"They had the furniture in the living room pushed out of the way and were slow dancing to something on the record player. I remember thinking how cute they looked together."

"So, umm, you wanna hit the dance floor?" He looked at her with a flirty, and sheepish grin.

"I'd like that. Yes"

Matt stood up before offering a hand to her. The contrast of hers with its well-manicured nails and his big, work roughened hands struck her hard. She really was out of her element with Matthew MacInnes.

He led her away from their table before pulling her into his arms. Smooth. Effortless. They glided together, even as he eased her tighter against him. The sensuous jazz notes wrapped around them, causing everything to fade away except the man holding her close.

She was falling for him so fast. Her sensible side screamed at her to slow down, pointing out she barely knew him. And yet, that little inner voice, the one she always relied on for tough decisions, urged her on. *Go for it.*

A smattering of applause rippled through the crowd at the end of the music, pulling Suz back into reality. While they'd been on the dance floor, twilight had tiptoed into the evening. Once back at their table, she draped the cardigan she'd brought, just-in-case, around her shoulders.

"Are you too chilly? Should we leave?" Matt asked, a concerned look clouding his face.

Suz shook her head. "I'm good if you are." She looked around. "They're lighting the propane heaters. Unless you want to go."

"No. I'm good, too."

They settled back at their table, enjoying the rest of their dinner and the lovely music. When the band took another break, she and Matt decided it would be a good time to head out.

As they walked along the sidewalk, Matt threaded his fingers through her own. holding her hand. In response, Suz leaned in closer and, for just a split second, rested her head against his shoulder.

The ride back to her place, even within the quiet and comfort of a long-time friendship, reinforced in her mind that things *were* different now. She and Matt were dating.

\# \# \#

Matt pulled the VW to a halt in her driveway and shut the engine off. "You know I'm going to walk you to the door, don't you?"

Suz smiled. "Knowing your family, I have no doubt."

Out of the corner of his eye, Matt saw her gaze follow him as he went around to open her door, checking him out—just like he'd done with her earlier at the restaurant. Damned if it didn't feel good. *Real good.*

He wrapped his arm around her waist as they walked up to her door. Once there, she turned to face him before bringing his other arm around her, and then stepped into an embrace before he knew what was happening.

"I had an absolutely fabulous time, Matt," Suz wrapped her arms around him as she spoke. She cuddled closer, her breasts pressing against his chest.

The woman sure knew how to reinforce a comment.

"Me, too." He repositioned slightly in an attempt to keep her from discovering his thickening cock. But to no avail, for she maneuvered them so that her thigh wedged between his.

Taking her actions as an almost invitation, Matt slid his hands down from her waist to cup both rounded ass cheeks. Her appreciative moan was all the approval he needed before giving her backside a gentle but unmistakable squeeze.

"Matt, as much as I think we both want more, it's too early for a bedroom romp." She pulled back a bit.

"I know that up here." He tapped a finger against his temple.

Her hand reached up to caress his face, fingertip trailing across his lips. "Well, know this, too. We're going to end up there, sooner rather than later." She brought her other hand up and wrapped her arms around his neck. "Now, kiss me goodnight before my resolve weakens."

He barely let her get the words out of her mouth before he captured her lips then wedged his tongue between them, demanding entrance. She tasted the bourbon apple crisp they'd shared for dessert. Matt teased her, in and out, until Suz began sucking on his tongue. His mind immediately imagined how good it would feel if she were sucking his cock.

A low, breathy moan escaped her lips, reassuring him that she was just as into this as he. Encouraged by her obvious approval, he nipped at her bottom lip

"Dear heavens, Matt. We gotta stop."

He eased back a little bit but didn't completely let her go. "Yeah, while we can." Matt eased his hold on her, allowing her to take a step backward.

Suz licked her lips, now reddened due to more than her lipstick and swollen from his kisses. "You taste good." She gave him a quick peck on one cheek. "I'm going in now. Dream naughty," she added with a flirtatious wink before disappearing inside.

Matt walked back to the car, still a bit gobsmacked. A relationship with this woman was going to be so very different from anything he'd ever experienced. Her living room light flicked off as he fastened his seat belt. Unable to resist the urge to do a bit more flirting himself, he swiped the screen of his phone into life. Several keystrokes later, he tapped the send button, and then smiled to himself as he started up the engine and backed out of the drive. "That should make sure *she* dreams naughty, too."

# # #

Judge Barnes picked her way along the cracked and occasionally broken concrete walkway that ran alongside the flower beds. *Mother's flowers.* What was left of them, anyway. The last two rose bushes would need to be pruned back before the coming winter and the spring bulb bed would need to be tucked in with dry leaves or straw.

Madeline had helped her mother plant those roses the summer she'd turned thirty. The summer Winslow had told her the awful truth before walking out of her life forever. The truth behind her father's shrinking fortune. And the role the MacInnes clan had been playing for decades.

She pulled the pruning shears from one of the deep pockets of her apron. Snipping away, she gathered the last of this season's mint and basil before trimming back the stragglers in the patch of perennials.

"Heavens, how did you survive this long?" She spotted a straggler foxglove. "You should've been long gone by July." As she cut, an idea formed in her mind, a smile lighting her face. "Yes, and I know just the time and place."

#

"No, no. Stop!" Marianne put a finger in each ear. "La, la, la, la. I can't hear you. La, la, la, la. TMI, way TMI."

Suz couldn't help but laugh. "You said you wanted to know."

"I expected something sweet, kinda mushy. Not how my cousin wanted to bonk my best friend's brains out."

"You wanted all the deets." Suz kept the info to herself on the phone sex that had followed the very explicit text message. "I need to finish up lunch." She trailed the last French fry through the remnants of her ketchup puddle before popping it into her mouth. "I'm meeting Gray to go over the menu plans for the Halloween party some of the Bourbon Women booked in the event center."

"I saw that on his calendar. He's working on something, and I quote, caramel appley." Marianne polished off her own lunch. "That reminds me. You doing anything for Sunday brunch?"

Suz thought for a moment and then shook her head. "Nope. What ya got in mind?"

"Colin's friend Hank just got engaged to his girlfriend Charlotte, and they're coming up this weekend. Thought we'd celebrate. Nothing big, just them, Colin and Jenni, Gray and I, plus you and Matt if you want to join us."

Were she and Matt a couple now? *After just one date?*

"Kinda coupley, ain't it?"

"Seems like it, doesn't it? Guess it just turned out that way." Marianne gathered up both her and Suz's trays and carried them over to the dish room window. Back at their table, Marianne grabbed her wallet. "I need to get back, we're pulling an experimental batch this afternoon." Suz nodded, looping the strap of her purse over one shoulder. "Anyway, check with Matt and let me know. It's gonna be out at Colin's, though Gray and I are doing the cooking."

After saying their goodbyes, Suz got in her car and headed down the drive to Gray's office at the event center. Once there, she met up with the distillery's new chef, and Marianne's watch dog. They spend the better part of two hours talking over the party menu and drink pairings.

"You have a great knack for working the distillery's different bourbons into the menu," Suz stated, impressed.

"I try." He shrugged and grinned.

She closed her notebook and then shoved it into her tote bag. "Thanks for making time to talk over the food. I'll send your proposed menu over to the planning committee. I'm sure they'll approve it. I sure would."

"Hey, before you go, you doing okay?"

Her stomach tightened. *Should I tell him? Or act all cool?* She quickly decided to lay a few of her emotional cards on the table. "To be honest, it shook me to the core."

"Sleeping?" His tone was the one of someone who'd been in the same situation.

"Yes," she paused, "and no. I've had a couple of bad dreams."

"I bet you have. Have you talked to Matt about it?" He stood from his chair.

"No. I don't want him to worry," she replied as she shook her head. "Should I?"

Gray leaned back and half sat on the edge of his desk. "Consider this. As a Marine, he saw more than his fair share of combat. He knows what its like to be shot at. And I would bet he's had his fair share of bad dreams. I sure have. Colin, too."

"I don't know." Did she dare? *Would it change what ever it was the two of them had going?*

"Trust him. If he's the man I think he is, you won't regret it." He pushed away from his desk to stand back up.

She rose from her seat. "Thanks, Gray. I'll think about it, I promise."

"Don't wait too long. They can go from bad dreams to nightmares very easily."

Gray's words echoed in her head as she walked out to her SUV. She had very definite plans for taking Matt to bed, soon—and waking up in the middle of the night, crying or screaming from a nightmare, would not be cool the first time with a new guy.

Especially not one like Matthew MacInnes.

Maybe, though, Gray might be right. She pulled her phone from the oversized bag that served both as her purse and computer bag slash briefcase. Scrolling through her contacts list, she found the name. The call rang several times before switching over to voicemail.

"Hey, Matt, it's Suz." *No shit, Sherlock. The man knows who's calling.* "Listen, give me a call when you get a few minutes. I've got something I need to talk to you about. Umm, thanks."

# # #

Matt walked up to the counter at his favorite local gun shop. "Hey, Mike. Steve. Y'all having a good day?"

Both men nodded. "We're closing in on deer season and I've already had to reorder three-oh-eight," Mike, the owner, said.

"And you just hate the sound of another sale ringing up, don't ya?"

"It just breaks this good ol' Kentucky boy's heart." Mike clutched dramatically at his chest. "What can we do for you today?"

"Just stopped by to see if my new scope has come in." Matt squatted down to see the pistols on the lower shelf of the glass case.

"We got a late UPS delivery yesterday that I didn't get a chance to unpack. It might be in there." Mike headed back toward the office. "Steve, show Matt that Glock we took as a trade in yesterday."

Matt watched the clerk take a beefy looking automatic pistol from one of the other cases. Steve ejected the magazine and then pulled back the slide before locking it in place. He then handed it over.

Once he'd given a quick look to verify the chamber was empty, Matt released the slide. "This one of the forties they came out with a couple of years ago?" he asked

Steve nodded. "Dude traded it in on a Kimber."

"To each their own." The pistol didn't sit well in his grip. "Too boxy," he said as he set it down on the gun rug. "I'll stick with my Springfield forty-five."

"You're in luck, Matt. That scope did come in that shipment." Mike came back out into the shop. He set the box on the counter. "Need mounting rings?"

Matt shook his head. "The ones I've got should work."

While Mark wrote up the bill for Matt, Sheriff Whitaker walked into the shop. "Mornin' Mike, Steve. Did that special order ammo come in yet?"

"Sure did, Dave." Mike looked up. "It's in the ammo locker. Steve, would you get the sheriff's order?"

Whitaker glanced over at Matt and nodded in recognition. "MacInnes," he said, his greeting all business.

"Sheriff," Matt responded in kind. Dave Whitaker had always rubbed him the wrong way. Nothing in particular to point a finger at, just the wrong sort of vibe for the highest-ranking law enforcement officer in the whole county.

Steve returned, setting two boxes on the counter. "Hundred and seventy-five grain, Match King hollow points."

Opening the box on top, Whitaker removed one bullet, looking it over. "Got a match in Lexington this weekend. There's a retired officer from Nashville that's been a thorn in my side at competitions for years. I plan to send him back to Tennessee with a butt whoopin' score." He pulled a credit card from his wallet and tossed it onto the counter. "Ring it up, Steve."

Matt stood there as the uncomfortable silence grew into the elephant in the room. Unable to tolerate it any longer, he decided to prod Sheriff Whitaker. "How's the investigation going?"

"Haven't really heard much. That female from the Staties is running the show."

Matt bit back a rebuttal. From what he'd seen, Jessica Kent was a fine investigator. More than that, a caring and friendly person. The exact sort of person he wanted to be figuring out just what the hell was going on with MacInnes Distillery. And more importantly, who was behind the shooting.

"Say, MacInnes, how's that girl doing?"

"What girl?" Matt knew exactly who the sheriff meant. But this was a chance to dig back against the other man's rude comment.

"The one you were with when the shooting happened."

"In case you haven't noticed, most grown women don't appreciate being called a girl, especially by a man in your official position. If I were you, I'd start using woman, or even lady." Matt scooped up his package. "But to answer your question, Suz Benton is doing well. Very, very well in my opinion."

Chapter 4

Suz had to smile when the screen on her phone lit up with Matt's name. "Hi."

"How ya doing?"

She had it bad. His voice alone had her heart racing. "Been busy, and got stuff done."

"Me, too."

Once she'd backed out of the parking space, she drew in a deep breath to gather her nerves. "So, umm, the reason I left you that message."

The line went quiet for a long moment of silence. So long, she was afraid that either the call had dropped or he'd hung up on her.

"I want to talk. To tell you something. But its gotta be in person."

"Oh?"

She could hear the questioning, the catch, the concern in his voice. "Don't worry. It's nothing bad—well, not really."

"You have to explain that."

An idea formed in her mind. "Anything planned for tonight?"

"Repainting the cabinets in my kitchen. You any good with a paint brush?"

"I can rock a paintbrush. How about I pick up subs or pizza or something? We can paint, then have dinner and talk."

"No way am I going to turn down help." He paused and took a drink of something. "As far as dinner, sure. Grab whatever sounds good. I'm not picky. Just come on over. I'll be home about four."

"Cool. Text me your address to make sure I have it."

Suz stared at her phone even after they'd hung up. *There, that went well, didn't it?* Now all she had to do was get her courage up enough to tell Matt about her nightmares.

I can do that. Right?

# # #

"So, this used to be your Aunt Muriel's house?"

Matt nodded as he led Suz through the living and dining rooms, and on into the kitchen. "She's actually a great aunt, my MacInnes grandfather's sister. Moved to Florida a couple of years ago after Uncle Charlie passed. I bought it and have slowly been remodeling and updating ever since."

She set the bag of chips and sandwiches, along with her purse, on the big, farm-style table at one end of the room. "Let's eat first. I'm starved."

"Good idea." Matt opened the fridge. "Let's see. I've got sodas, a pitcher of lemonade, water." His voice trailed off. "And some mismatched beers." He peered around the open door. "I have eclectic tastes."

"The lemonade sounds great. I love a good pucker."

From the look on his face, her flirty comment must've caught him off guard. For a second, his jaw dropped open, but no words came out. He recovered fast. "Lemonade it is."

Suz spied two tall glasses in the dish drainer. "I'll put ice in these."

As the cubes clinked into the glasses, Matt added, "There's chips in the pantry through that door." He pointed toward the far end of the room. "Paper plates, too."

They got dinner set up in just a few minutes, sitting at one end of the kitchen table.

"I got all the upper doors off and ready out on the back porch. There must have been at least half a dozen layers of paint on those things. Even with the chemical stripper, it took me almost a week working in my spare time."

"How old is the house?" Sus asked before she bit into her sub sandwich.

"Turn of the century. Hence all the high ceilings."

"It's gorgeous." *Stop stalling.* She crunched into a couple of chips before washing them down with the lemonade.

"It's a work in progress is what it is. I'm planning to rip up this flooring and put in some nice laminate." He set his sandwich down. "You wanted to talk about something?"

"Yeah, I did." She wiped a smear of mayo from her lips. "I've had a couple of bad dreams since we were shot at."

Matt leaned back in his chair. "I'm not surprised." He paused for a bit and then asked, "How bad?"

She told him about the first dream. "It was like a replay of how it all happened, only scarier."

"And the other one?"

"It was worse." Suz described how it started out the same as the first, but that the shots just kept coming. And they were also locked out of the event center, without anyone to help. "I woke up in a cold sweat, I was so scared."

Leaning closer to the table, he reached out to hold her hand. "And all completely normal. Your mind is processing an event you had no preparation to cope with. At least that's what they taught us in the Corps."

"Do you . . . umm ever . . ."

He nodded. "Every once in a while, yeah. And nowhere near as often as right after my first deployment."

"So, what do I do?"

"For one thing, exactly what you're doing now. Talk to someone who understands. A therapist or counsellor." He took a drink from his glass. "Or me."

"You'd do that? Even in the middle of the night?"

"Hell, yes. You can also look up grounding exercises online. They can help you, how was it they told us?" Matt paused as if trying to find the right word, "Help you to reconnect your mind back into the real world." He gave her thigh a squeeze.

Suz covered his hand with hers. "I really appreciate that, Matt," she said, polishing off the last bite of her sub sandwich. "Now let's get those cabinet doors painted."

# # #

With both of them working, the doors sat propped up to dry on the back porch in no time. So quickly in fact, they started with the front of the upper cabinets. At nearly ten o'clock, they rinsed out their brushes and folded up the drop cloth covering the kitchen's tiled floor.

Suz reached up to trail her fingers across the front of his tee shirt, then gripped the front, before giving it a tug. "Walk me to my car."

"Gladly."

She scooped up her purse and jacket as they walked through the living room. Matt pushed the front door open.

"You know, I might be dating you for this porch alone," she quipped.

It still needed some cosmetic sprucing up, but the porch itself was solid. He'd obviously replaced some of the floorboards with new wood, along with a few of the spindles supporting the railing. But the porch itself looked lived in. Inviting. The perfect place for a sunny afternoon with a good book or the first cup of morning coffee as the neighborhood revved up for a busy day.

"Just for my porch, huh?"

"There might be a few other reasons." She trailed her fingers down one t-shirt covered shoulder to biceps honed by hours of physical work in the distillery's cooperage. "Then again, it could just be your charming self."

"Well in that case..." Matt gripped her arms and pulled her close then captured her mouth with his.

The kiss pushed right past gentle and dove straight into toe-curling deliciousness. He nipped at her bottom lip until she granted him entrance. Their tongues dueled back and forth, teasing and swirling. He still tasted of the apple pie they'd shared once the painting was done, with hints of bourbon and cinnamon.

His hands slid down over her back to cup both cheeks of her backside, caressing and squeezing. And making her so very wet as she squirmed against him.

Finally, he pulled away with a knowing, self-satisfied smile on his handsome face. "You okay to drive home?"

Suz nodded. "You haven't kept me up that far past my bedtime."

He cocked his head to one side. "You know what I meant."

She laced her fingers with his and tugged him down the steps toward her car. "I know. And just so you know, my B.O.B. is going to get a workout later."

"Bob?" he asked, his face clouded by confusion.

Suz giggled as she leaned in close and whispered, "Battery operated boyfriend."

Matt rolled his eyes at her before gently kissing her forehead once she unlocked the door. "Call me. I want to listen to you come hard while you talk to me."

She let a low and throaty moan escape her lips. "Yes, sir."

# # #

The Friday afternoon sun cast long shadows on the floor of Suz's office. She tapped her pen on the yellow notepad. "Absolutely, ma'am. I can make sure you're placed next to Sheriff Whitaker at the head table."

"Wonderful," Judge Barnes replied. "I want to endorse his candidacy. I feel it will be better for photo ops if I'm seated beside him at the banquet."

"We can definitely make that happen, Judge. Your support has gotten him into office two times and I'm sure this time will be no different." She drew a rectangle on the page for the table, scribbling *Judge* to the left of *Sheriff*. "Do you have any preferences for the menu?"

"Anything but that awful rubber chicken so many of these eventsserve." Judge Barnes paused a moment. "Oh, and a nice side salad. Something green and crisp."

No rubber chicken and add green side salad. Suz added to her notes on this event. "That's an easy request. I'll send the final menu over to you for approval in the next couple of days if that's okay with you."

"That will be fine, dear. It's so nice to work with a professional organizer. I'm glad I had a chance to meet you at the MacInnes Distillery before that awful shooting. I do hope you're doing well."

"Thank you. Yes, I'm fine."

Suz wrapped up the call and then jotted down the last of her call notes along with a quick email to the caterer. This was the fifth event she'd booked from contacts she'd made on that day. It almost made getting shot at worth it. Almost. That, and literally pushing Matthew MacInnes into her lap.

Well, not exactly her lap. One minute they'd been calmly chatting out on the patio. The next, she'd found herself sprawled on the floor with him pressed across her back. The pure, masculine muscle of him had sent her imagination and fantasies into hyperdrive. She'd seen the man shirtless many times, both working in the cooperage and playing cornhole at the recent distillery picnic.

Now that she knew the thick size of his erection, admittedly through his jeans, she couldn't keep from imagining just how good it would feel—having him so deep inside her, stretched tight.

Stop that. Getting all hot and bothered here at work was not cool at all. Besides, she giggled, all her toys were at home.

Somehow, she managed to keep her mind focused to the projects, talking with clients, reaching out to venues, contracting caterers, D.J.s and bands. She loved her work, fitting all the pieces together to make a successful event. But damn, it had been so long since she'd been this jazzed over a new man in her life. Maybe not ever.

When she finally managed to head across the street to where she'd parked her SUV, the church bells down the block were chiming six o'clock. Her belly rumbled, reminding her that lunch had been an apple and a carton of yogurt eaten on the run hours ago between phone calls.

Suz picked up her phone once she sat behind the wheel, thinking she'd give Matt a call about dinner before remembering he wasn't going to be home until late. They'd talked on the phone over coffee this morning, when he'd told her he had to go over to Benton to pick up some special staves for a presentation barrel he had to build.

"In that case," she spoke out loud. "guess I'll have to eat a pulled pork sandwich alone." So she called her favorite 'que place to order a pound of meat, a tub of their house-made potato salad, "And a bottle of your Carolina mustard sauce. I'm out at home."

"Curbside or you want to come in?"

"Inside. The smells are part of the whole experience."

# # #

After a meal of pulled pork and mustard potato salad consumed while watching a sexy little rom-com on her tablet, Suz headed to the bathroom for some further self-indulgent time. The new bottle of lavender scented bath oil and her scrubby puff had left her skin soft and glowing. And admittedly with wrinkled fingertips because she'd soaked until the water had begun to go chilly.

Once she'd climbed out of the tub and dried off, she shrugged into a short robe and walked barefoot into the kitchen. A cup of chamomile tea with a dollop of honey would complete her evening of relaxation. Tea in hand, Suz made a final pass through the house—lights off and doors locked.

A fresh pair of panties and the long tee shirt from under her pillow later, she slid between the soft flannel sheets. "Where was I?" Opening to the bookmarked page, Suz found the right spot. "Ah, yes, the train ride from London to Oxford." She snuggled down against the pillows, ready for an adventure.

# # #

The late summer breeze brought not only dust, but also the carnival scents of hot fry oil, sugary cotton candy, and caramel corn as it fluttered the full skirt of her sundress. Suz strolled along beside Matt, past the carousel and bumper cars.

Without a word, Matt headed down the row of booths with games of skill and chance. They walked past the crowd of youngsters crowded around the duck pickup. The same with the oldsters tossing coins onto glass plates. He finally led her to the booth featuring a sharp-shooting challenge.

The man running the booth handed Matt one of the rifles. He worked the lever, just like the guns on those old westerns before raising the weapon to his shoulder and taking the shot. The pellet struck one of the little bell targets with a ping. A sparkly pinwheel on a long plastic stick was unceremoniously plunked down as a prize.

A second rifle was thrust into Suz's hands as Matt took a second shot. This time, his pellet popped one of the many balloons scattered over the board of targets, sending a poof of scarlet red glitter into the humid summer air.

Her hands shaking, she followed Matt's example and worked the action on the rifle, bringing into shooting position. Unsure exactly how to aim, she pointed the barrel toward the slowly turning wheel with tin cutouts of ducks on the edge. Her pellet pinged against one of the ducks.

That's when it started. No prize and no red glitter, but a trickle of scarlet liquid from the spot where the metal duck had stood. She fired again, knocking over a second duck. It, too, caused a stream of red to flow down the wheel.

Beside her, Matt fired in rapid succession, hitting target after target. With each one he brought down, scarlet splattered over the booth.

Suz touched the splatters that had landed on her skin and clothes. Warm. Sticky. Oh my God. It's blood. *Her throat and stomach spasmed in concert.*

And yet, she couldn't stop the fascination and desire for more. So she, too, started rapid firing. Each metal target she hit spurted more blood. Soon, the three of them, Matt, the man running the game, and Suz herself were covered in scarlet red gore.

Shot after shot, they fired not only at the targets, but the stuffed animal prizes. All of them bleeding. Dripping, oozing. Spurting. A blood bath, right there at the carnival.

"No, no!" *she screamed.* "Matt. Stop!"

Suz tried to drop the gun in her hands, but she couldn't get it to let go. The weapon was stuck in her grip, cemented there by all the bloody gore. Try as she could, her hold would not release. In a vain attempt, she tried using her gun to knock the one from Matt's hands. It, too, was stuck fast. He kept firing and firing until he turned the gun onto the man running the game.

His movement slowed as he brought the weapon up into position again. She watched as the muscles in his finger slowly squeezed down on the trigger.

"Matt, noooooooooooooooooooooooo!"

She startled awake, sitting bolt upright in bed—sobbing, tears streaming down her cheeks, and shaking like she had a raging fever. Once the fog from the dream began to clear, she could hear herself repeating, "Just a dream, just a dream," over and over.

Her breath in ragged gasps, she managed to crawl to the edge of the bed. Suz reach over to the bedside table and grabbed her phone. With fingers still trembling, she managed to find the number of the one person she thought might be able to help.

One ring. Second ring. Third ring. *Come on. Answer. Please.*

"Hullo."

"M-M-Matt." She sniffled her way through just saying his name.

"Suz?" The sleepiness disappeared from his voice.

"I, umm," she swiped away the tears from her eyes, "I had another dream."

"I'll be right there."

Twenty minutes later, every light in the house was on. She had her fingers wrapped around a mug of hot herbal tea and her hands were finally steady, while her heart rate had settled down.

The distinctive motor sound of Matt's VW pulled to a stop outside. She headed to the door, to get the lock and chain undone and the door opened just in time for him to step up to the storm door.

Wordlessly, he stepped inside and gathered her into his arms. She let herself collapse against his broad chest. Within seconds, her searing hot tears began flowing again. As she sobbed against him, she heard him kick her front door closed.

Matt placed one hand against her back and threaded the other through her hair. "Hold on," he whispered, then scooped her up and carried her over to the couch, settling her across his lap.

Slowly, she managed to pull herself together. Getting a tissue from the box on the coffee table, she blotted at her eyes and blew her nose. "Sorry for interrupting your sleep."

He kissed her, soft and sweet, on the cheek. "Never apologize about reaching out for help, sweetheart. Especially from me."

"It was so damn real."

Matt brushed the hair from her face as he nodded. "They usually are, those dreams so rooted in real events." He stroked down the side of her face. "Wanna tell me about it?"

Do I? Do I really want to rehash that nightmare? Suz nodded. "I think I do. But I want to do it snuggled up against you. In my bed."

She swore that every muscle in his body tightened. Had she completely misread all of his words and actions? Didn't he want to sleep curled up beside her? "Something wrong?" she asked him, dreading his answer.

She could almost hear his thoughts forming from the look on his face.

"Nothing's wrong. I just want you to be sure of one thing. I do want you, in the most physical way. But tonight is about support and chasing away those nightmares. You take your tea and head on to the bedroom. I'll turn off all of the lights and lock the front door before I join you."

What she wanted to hear the most...

A girl could easily fall for this man. *Maybe I've already started to...*

# # #

Light from the full moon streamed in through Suz's bedroom window as Matt listened to her rhythmic breathing. She'd finally fallen asleep about an hour ago after she'd spun out her nightmare for him.

This one had ranked right up there with some of his own nocturnal replays. His had always been more realistic, but he'd easily made the connection between the actual event and her horrible, graphic nightmare. She's held it together for the first part of the story, yet she'd sobbed against his bare chest the bloodier the tale had gotten.

He speculated that her subconscious had set the shooting against a carnival scene since that was likely the only experience she'd had with guns. From what she'd told him on their date, she was a city girl through and through.

Maybe. An idea began to take shape in his mind. Maybe if he taught her the skills to safely fire a gun, if she learned to control one, the new skill would help calm down her dreams. That was something he could do to help. Something more concrete.

Not that coming over when she'd called wasn't useful. The relieved look on her face when she'd opened her front door to let him in had completely dispelled that worry. But this would be more proactive, maybe keep future dreams away.

Satisfied that he had a plan brewing, Matt snuggled back down next to her, spooning up to her backside. That sweet ass, in just a tiny pair of bikini panties, was driving his cock crazy. But hell, he figured she'd already realized he'd been hard most of the evening with her.

So, he slid one arm up under her pillow before he draped the other around her waist and tugged her close. He got rewarded with a sleepy moan and half smile.

"Goodnight, sweetheart." He kissed her cheek.

"Night." Her voice was raspy with sleep.

He'd start putting his plan in motion tomorrow. Well, later today, actually. For now though, snuggling with his girl and drifting off to sleep sounded like a mighty fine thing.

His girl. *Yeah, I like that.*

Chapter 5

Judge Barnes scuffed her way across the kitchen floor in her oldest slippers. Once she'd poured a cup of coffee, she headed back to her desk. No one was going to believe what she had planned.

The only thing that would make the plan better would be some fresh leaves and her homemade tincture to go into a salad. She knew the man to be a robust eater, so he was sure to clean his plate. All she had was her dried supply.

Already putting her secret plan in motion, she'd arranged to sit next to him at the announcement dinner. She'd have plenty of opportunity to spike his meal.

Everybody would be none the wiser. She'd be so sneaky, her additions going unnoticed. She could add the crumbled up, dried leaves, or drops of the tincture. Not a soul would see.

She'd get away with this one. Just like she had in the past. No one ever suspected the beloved judge. Even if anyone were to dare to suspect, no one could prove it. Because, in her whole life, no one had been able to pin anything on Madelyn Barnes.

Yesterday, she'd put her plan in motion. That gullible, young woman had accepted every suggestion Madelyn had made—even making sure to arrange the seating to put her right next to the sheriff. This would be no challenge.

Madelyn had to smile. Granny would never have imagined how the plant knowledge she'd shared with her curious granddaughter would eventually be used. It was going to help Madelyn once again to solve a problem.

Oh yes, this was going to come in handy one more time.

"Matt. It's me." Suz's voice called out along with a rap on the screen door.

"Come on in. It's not locked." He'd left the big door open, leaving just the screen, specifically so he'd hear her arrive. Heading out from the kitchen at the back of the house, he caught up to her and pulled her in for a kiss.

Her scent, light and citrusy, mixed with the minty taste of her toothpaste, never failed to drive him more than a little crazy. And the memory of waking up beside her yesterday morning... hell, he'd been half hard ever since.

"Morning, sweet thing."

She moaned. "I missed you."

"It's barely been twenty-four hours," he said with a grin.

She eased out of his hug and shrugged, a self-satisfied smile on her face. "You ready to go?"

"Just let me straighten this mess up." He sat on the edge of the couch to gather up a jumbled pile of papers and old photos.

One fluttered to the floor. Suz scooped it up. "Who are these kids?"

He took the picture she handed over. "Well, that's my dad." He pointed to the younger of the two preteen boys. "That," he said, pointing to the other boy, "is Uncle Jim. Colin and Marianne's dad."

"What about her? She looks like she's about, oh, fourteen, maybe fifteen..."

Matt nodded. "About that, yeah. And I have no idea who she is. A neighbor kid maybe. Or some visiting distant cousin. I've been going through stuff I've found cleaning out closets and the attic. I mentioned that this place belonged to my Great Aunt Muriel, right?"

"Yeah. So, what are you gonna do with them?"

"Don't tell anyone, but I'm thinking about making a photo album for both Dad and Uncle Jim for Christmas. I'm going to see if either Colin or Marianne know anything about the girl in that picture."

"That's a cool idea."

He finished straightening things up, tapping the papers on the coffee table before setting the stack down. "There. Now let's head out." He put his hand on the small of her back once they stood up, gently guiding her to the door. "And yes, before you ask, I'm driving."

# # #

Suz had heard Marianne talk about the building her brother Colin was turning into a home. It had been the old co-op, selling livestock feed and supplies to the local farmers. In fact, the over-sized scale still hung where the kitchen space merged into the great room. But this was the first time she'd been inside.

"There's just something about fire and grilling that draws men to it, isn't there?" Suz turned away from looking out the glass doors out to where all four of the men stood around the grill. "You can almost see the caveman in all of them."

All three of the other ladies laughed along with her as she reclaimed her tall seat at what would be called a breakfast bar, enabling guests to chat with whoever was doing the cooking.

"Anyone need a refill on wine?" Jenni, Colin's fiancée, held up the open bottle in invitation.

Handing her glass over, Charlotte said, "I'm not driving, I'll take some." While her glass was being refilled, she swiveled her seat to face Suz. "I heard about the shooting. Are you doing all right?"

"Yes and no." Suz took a sip from her own glass. "During the day, I'm okay. But, I admit, I've been having some bad dreams. Guess my mind still needs time to process the whole thing,"

"Charlotte's going to write a big article about all the threats that have been made against the women connected to the bourbon industry," Marianne added as she stirred the chopped onions sizzling on the big cast iron skillet. "She interviewed me."

"And me," Jenni added as she handed the refilled wine glass back to Charlotte.

"I'm hoping you'll agree to talk with me, too, Suz. I know Colin thinks there is a possibility the shooter mistook you for Marianne, but you were still the one out there on that patio when the shot was fired."

"You both agreed, and think it's okay? I don't want to say or do anything to hurt the MacInnes brand."

Marianne shook her head. "You'll do fine. Charlotte's trying to focus on the women's stories in all of this."

"I'm not even going to publish anything until this is all over and the case is solved. I defiantly don't want to do anything to interfere with Detective Kent's case."

Suz mulled it over for a moment or two. "All right, we can set something up." She picked up the wine bottle before pouring the last of the beverage into her glass. "Now that we have that settled, let's get back to the reason for the party. Let me see that ring."

# # #

"I like Colin's friends." Suz shed her cardigan before draping it over the back of the overstuffed armchair in Matt's living room. "Charlotte told me the whole story about the huge chance she took trying to get an interview with Hank."

"Hank makes some quality bourbon, too. I've got a bottle of his Briar Jumper on my bourbon shelf right now."

Suz plopped down on the couch, leaning back and spreading her arms wide. "So, we've got the rest of the afternoon and evening at our disposal. What ya wanna do?" She gave him what she hoped was her best saucy wink. "Wanna make out?"

"You know, don't you, that it will probably go farther than just making out?" Matt took the few steps toward her until he stood beside the couch. "I doubt either of us will want to stop."

She grinned up at him. "I'm kinda counting on that."

A deep rumbling growl escaped Matt's lips. The cushion dipped with the weight of his knee before he leaned over her, bracing his hands on the couch behind her as he brought his mouth down on hers.

Reaching up, Suz slid her arms around his neck, her fingertips brushing his military short haircut. She opened her lips and slid her tongue into his mouth. He still tasted faintly of the cinnamon apple dessert they'd all raved about.

Matt moved, easing down beside her as their tongues kept on playing the advance and retreat game, teasing and tasting back and forth. Once he'd settled beside her, he pulled her over to sit across his lap, allowing her to cuddle into his arms.

His kisses turned into nibbles on her lower lip, while she let her hands roam over his neck and shoulders. She'd longed to touch him for so very long—no way was she going to rush to the bedroom. But to really enjoy this, Suz was going to have to divest him of the flannel shirt he'd worn over to the brunch.

Meanwhile, Matt untucked her blouse skillfully from her jeans. Just as expertly, he slid one hand under the fabric, gliding it over her skin and up to the front closure of her bra. With a deft flick, he had the fastener undone.

"Oh, yes," she moaned, giving him clear permission to continue.

Still working under her buttoned-up blouse, Matt pushed the bra cups off to the sides, exposing her breasts to both his touch and the feel of the soft cotton fabric. Her nipples had always been extremely responsive, but this delightful sensation threatened to drive her to climax right then and there.

"Oh, you like that, do you, sweetheart?" The self-satisfied, masculine cockiness was so obvious in his voice.

She drew in a deep, ragged breath, yet attempted to tamp down her response. "Yes, Matt. I love it. And I want more. Lots more." She gripped the front of his shirt. "I want," she popped one of the buttons free, "skin," then pushed a second one loose, "on skin."

Once she had the shirt part way open, her fingers teased their way onto his chest. The instant she touched his flesh, the hard ridge of his cock twitched under her ass.

As she teased and explored, Matt toyed with her hardened nipples, circling around and around over the crinkled skin of her areola. His fingers sent shivers of sensations right down to her clit as he began to kiss and nip his way down her neck and then up to her ear.

"The blouse has to go, sweet thing."

"So does your shirt. I want to feel my tits against your bare chest."

A low growl rumbled in Matt's chest as he pushed her fingers away from the buttons. "I want to uncover those myself." He made quick work of opening her blouse before he pushed both it and her bra off her shoulders. "Simply gorgeous." He bent his head then circled one puckered nipple with the tip of his tongue. "Delicious, too. I must try the other."

The sensations he'd aroused were coursing their way down her body, straight to her clit. As he moved his mouth over to her other nipple, wetness gathered between her thighs and had her gripping his broad shoulders. A throaty moan escaped her lips just before she gasped out his name. "Yes, dear heavens, yes, Matt."

This time he sucked harder, his tongue stroking her nipple like a greedy babe. "If you don't stop, I'm gonna . . . gonna . . ."

"What, sweet thing?" He let his teeth gently rasp over the taut nipple. "What are you gonna do?"

She gripped him even tighter, not caring that tomorrow he might have fingertip-sized bruises. "You're going to make me come."

"That's my intent. I want you to give it to me. Do it, Suz. Give me a sample before I take you to bed. So you'll taste even sweeter when I dive between those thighs."

The image he put in her head pushed her over the orgasmic edge. Tiny muscles within her core began to quiver and spasm, making her ache to feel him touch and taste those soft and desire-slickened folds.

"Now. I want you. Want you hard and thick and deep inside me." She could hear the quivers in her voice as she begged him for what her body needed.

As he eased her from his lap, the ridge of his denim-covered erection rubbed up her backside. Reaching out and emboldened by the climax he'd just given her, she cupped his groin, giving it an appreciative gentle squeeze. "This. This is what I want, Matthew."

"Never let it be said that a MacInnes refused to give a lady what she wanted." He reached out and took her hand to lead her up the stairs to his bedroom.

The room, already getting dark in the late evening light coming in from the windows, was as unpretentious as the man who slept there. Matt tugged her along the hardwood floor, over to an antique brass bed.

He flipped the covers back before he pushed her back onto the sheets. "I'm going to take these off now." He gripped the button at the top of her zipper. Once it popped free of its confines, he tugged the tab slowly, tooth by frustrating tooth.

"Oh, dear Lord, Matt." Suz moaned as he peeled the denim down her legs.

He wandered a fingertip up one bare thigh and over the satiny fabric of her bikini panties.

"Aren't these pretty?" Matt hooked his fingers under the elastic band. "But they, too, must go. Lift that sweet ass." She braced her feet against the mattress and arched her butt up. He then tossed her panties to the floor. "Oh, what's this?" He touched her skin at the top of her right thigh. "Ink? Miss Benton has a tattoo?"

"Yes, I have a tattoo." Her cheeks warmed. "My spring break rebellion. Junior year."

He leaned in, close enough that his breath brushed against her skin. "Why, I do believe that's a strawberry ice cream cone. And, oh my, it's starting to drip. Right onto this sweet little pussy." Matt pressed a kiss against the small image. "Tasty. But looks like I need to lick up the drips."

With that, he circled the inked cone with the tip of his tongue, sending a shudder of electricity straight to those wet folds lower down. When his lips and tongue followed the same path, her whole body quivered in desire.

His tongue played up and down the seam between those folds before slipping in between and flicking over her clit. When he touched that uber sensitive bud, her hips arched up to press tighter against him.

"Matt!" she cried out while reaching down to push her fingers through his hair as she lowered her butt back onto the bed.

"Mmmm." His moan rumbled from somewhere deep within his chest. "Just as delicious as I thought you'd be. And much better," he licked up and down another time, "than any cone I've ever had."

His tongue stroked up and down over her wetness as she fought to hold back the rising tide of tension inside her—sliding over her slick inner flesh, Suz reached up, gripping one of the pillows and giving it a tight twist.

"Have mercy. Please. Please. I want you. I want that cock." She pulled in a ragged breath. "And I want it hard and balls deep. Now."

Seconds later, Matt's clothes had joined hers on the floor. The mattress dipped a bit as he planted his knee between her feet. His other knee brushing past her inner thigh, he settled his hips between her thighs.

As much as she longed for him to go on, she watched patiently as he rocked back onto his heels, leaned to open the bedside drawer, and reached inside, removing a small packet. In one deft move, he tore open the foil. Once he removed the condom, Matt tossed the wrapper aside and rolled the latex over his erection.

His gaze captured hers. "One last time, sweetheart. Tell me you want this."

"At this moment, Matthew, there is nothing I want more."

The second the words left her lips, Matt braced one hand beside her. With the other, he guided his cock toward her pussy and lowered his hips.

He slid in, hard and deep, just as she'd asked, then moved his hands to just above her shoulders, palms flat against the sheet. "Lock your legs around my ass," he whispered against her neck.

Spreading her thighs a bit wider, she did as he asked, hooking her ankles together. It gave her better leverage to match the rhythm he set. His shaft, thicker than her favorite toy, had her stretched tighter than she'd been in ... years. If ever.

It took all the control she could muster not to rake her fingernails hard down the muscled planes of his back. Instead, she gripped his shoulders, knowing there'd be a matching set of half-moon marks there in the morning.

"So damn good," he groaned against her ear. "Not gonna last long, sweetness."

"Me...neither, Matt." Suz pushed her hips harder against him, feeling him pressing even further into her depths. The knot of tension in her core wound tighter and tighter. Until finally, her control snapped.

"Matt!" she cried out as the inner spasms rolled through her in waves, stretching his name into a dozen syllables.

# # #

Propped up on one elbow, Matt watched the slow, rhythmic rise and fall of her breathing. Suz had created such a maelstrom of feelings and emotions in his head ... his gut. And his heart.

Yeah, my heart. That bit. Oh, sure, he'd been crushing on her off and on ever since Marianne had brought her along to the MacInnes Thanksgiving almost a decade ago. She'd floated in and out of his life on Marianne's coattails ever since, tiptoeing along the line between acquaintances and friends. Lately, though, he'd begun to see her in a different light.

Now here she was, sleeping in his bed, rousing every protective instinct he possessed. He wanted to be the one to chase away these nightmares. The one to keep her safe.

The only thing was, he needed a plan.

# # #

Suz looked over at Matt as they drove through town. "Are you sure about this?"

"I think so. Here's my logic," Matt replied as he pulled up to a stoplight. "You told me you've never been around guns or shooting. Right?"

"Yeah. Go on."

"I figure that since the dreams all involve the shooting, if you gain some experience and therefore more knowledge and control, you might not have any more of those nightmares." He shot her a quick glance before reaching out and giving her hand a squeeze. "If it doesn't work, there's other options. Either way, I got you."

Her heart skipped a beat. His *I got you* zinged past her brain and straight to her heart. She'd teetered on the brink of love a couple of times in the past. But now, she was desperately close to falling in love with this man.

Wearing safety glasses and ear-muff style hearing protection, Suz followed Matt through the heavy metal door on to the shooting range. He carried in two gun cases, one looking like a briefcase on steroids, the other obviously meant to hold rifles and such.

"Do you want to try a pistol or rifle first?" He flipped the latches open on the smaller case.

What do I want? She stepped closer. "What do you think?"

He cocked his head to one side. "Since the real shooting and your dreams all had rifles, I'd say start with this." Matt picked up one of the two in the case. "It's a twenty-two. It's what Dad started me out on. It's not heavy and doesn't kick much."

Suz reached out to take it from him, but just as she touched the rifle, he pulled it back. "What?"

"Hang on. There are four ironclad rules when it comes to shooting. First and foremost, never, ever point a gun at anything you aren't willing to destroy."

His voice had taken on a deathly serious tone, sending a shiver over her skin. She nodded. "And the other three?"

"Assume every gun is loaded until proven otherwise. Always make sure of your target, and what's behind it. Lastly, but just as important, keep your finger off the trigger until you are ready to shoot."

"I think I can remember those."

"Great. Let's get started."

# # #

"As always, pleasure doing business with you, Judge."

Madelyn Barnes sniffled back tears as she watched her grandmother's china cabinet being loaded onto the truck, where it joined the sideboard and dining room table with all of its chairs. Her family had celebrated innumerable birthdays, holidays, and anniversaries around that table. Debated critical decisions from those chairs.

"Here ya go." Bill Fischer ripped a check from the pad and handed it over. "I guess you're fixin' to sell this old place and move into one of those retirement condos in town."

Her throat tightened at the very suggestion of such a thing. But she knew the value of maintaining appearances. Madelyn nodded. "It's a shame I'm the last of the family. No one to bequeath these fine pieces to."

"They are quality. That's for sure." He climbed up into the cab of the big box truck where his two sons waited. "Thanks again for giving us a call, Judge."

She stood there at the front door, a single tear rolling down one cheek, watching the truck bounce down the hill toward the road on its way to I-75. Then back to Tennessee.

"I promise you, Granny," Madelyn said to the now empty dining room. "Those thieving MacInneses will pay for what I've had to do. They stole it. Stole Gran'pa's recipe. Made their fortune off of what they stole from us." She paced up and down the threadbare rug, her anger bubbling over. "Money that shoulda been ours."

Judge Barnes walked across the entryway into what had once been her grandfather's study. "Yes, they're going to pay. Oh, how they're going to pay." She picked up the corked bottle from where she'd left it on the desk when the Fischers had arrived. Once she'd unlocked the bottom drawer, she set the bottle carefully inside.

She gave the stopper a gentle pat before easing the drawer closed once again. "I do have a loose end to take care of first."

Chapter 6

Suz strolled along the sidewalk of the local shopping center along with Marianne. She stopped at one window. "Let's go in here."

"Oh. I like the powder blue," Marianne said.

"Gray's favorite color?" Suz nudged her friend with a gentle elbow to the ribs.

"I'll never tell." Marianne headed to the door. "Come on. This was your idea."

They shopped around for a few moments, until her friend stepped up beside her. "Find anything inter—"

"Hey, give that back."

Marianne waggled the scarlet scrap of satin and lace in Suz's face. "You." She paused, giving Suz's face the once over. "You've done it."

"Done what?" Suz grabbed the miniscule pair of panties, refolded them, and put them back in the stack. *Had Matt told his cousin? Otherwise, there was no way her friend could know that she'd slept with him.*

"*It.* The big it." When Suz didn't answer, Marianne leaned in closer. "Sex, you goof."

Suz prayed that the heat on her face wasn't showing in the store's lighting. "How'd you find out?"

Marianne rolled her eyes. "You just gave it away. Plus, you were looking at naughty undies. Nothing screams new lover like naughty lingerie."

#

When Suz arrived back home, her heart fluttered when she found a very familiar car parked out front and Matt sitting on her front steps. Carrying her shopping trip bags, she plopped down beside him. "Hey there, handsome."

"Evening, gorgeous." He leaned over and kissed her on the cheek.

"You're gonna make my neighbors think something's going on between us." She put her purse and the two bags down at her feet.

For a split second, Matt looked so confused, but then his face broke out in a huge grin. "Heaven forbid. We wouldn't want them to think that the two of us were fooling around or anything."

Giving him a wicked smile, Suz leaned across his lap and wrapped her arms around his neck. She pulled his face down to hers before kissing him hard and deep.

From across the street came a loud, crisp wolf whistle. Suz broke the kiss to look over her shoulder. Her neighbor, retired teacher Ruby Keeney, had hooked two fingers over her lips and let loose with the whistle.

When she sat back up, Suz wasn't sure how Matt would react to teasing by a total stranger. She'd heard him and Colin rib each other but this was different. But when she looked up at his face though, she was rewarded with a smile. He waved across the street at Ruby.

Ruby waved back then headed into her house with her grocery haul.

"Thanks for not getting upset. She's a great neighbor." She straightened up to sit beside him on the step. "What are you up to this afternoon?"

"I have to run down to the stave mill for a couple of days." Matt reached over and caressed her denim-covered thigh. "Wanted to make sure you knew where I was when I disappear for a bit."

"Just 'cause we had sex, you don't have to do that, Matt." But if she were honest with herself, she'd admit the idea that he wanted to warmed the very cockles of her heart. *Cockles, huh?*

His face clouded over. "You know me better than that. And yes, because we have. You're important, so I wanted you to know where I'm disappearing to."

Suz reached over and ran her hand down his face, her fingers stopping at his lips. Those cockles were about to burst into flames. She leaned in for a brief kiss—light and sweet like meringue on a pie. Pulling back, she sighed.

"Sorry, I was trying to be cool." She leaned her head on his shoulder. "We're still too new, Matt. I can't make any assumptions about us."

The weight of his arm settled around her shoulder. Warm, solid. And romantic.

"What assumption are you making?" He tugged her even tighter against his side.

She swallowed hard. "That maybe, sorta," she paused, gathering her thoughts, "that I, that we, well, could maybe be... a couple."

A laugh rumbled deep in his chest, bouncing her head against his shoulder. "Maybe?" He laughed again. "Trust me. We already are."

# # #

Detective Jessica Kent leaned against the door frame of her office, watching Sheriff Whitaker walk through the bull pen as she shook her head. "Jerk."

"Who?"

She turned toward the familiar voice of Dr. James Graham, Franklin County's Chief Medical Examiner and Jessica's long-time friend with benefits. Handsome, witty, and understood exactly how she liked her steak.

Jess Smiled. "To what do I owe this visit, Jim?" She turned back into the office, closing the door behind them.

"Who or what is jerking who around?"

She shrugged. "This whole MacInnes thing. Sheriff Whitaker showing up here every whip stitch. Says he's updating the mayor. Or the county council." She shook her head. "I'm being jerked around. And I don't f'n like it."

Jim nodded. "Don't blame you." He closed the blinds on the glass in her office door. "I came over to drop off some tox reports."

She rolled her eyes. "Jim, we both know those reports could've been sent through the computer system. It's even secure these days, ya know." Jess let the sarcasm drip a bit heavy off those last words.

"Guilty." He gave her the look of a kid with his hand caught in the cookie jar. "Can't I come over and see the prettiest detective in this part of the state just 'cause I want to?"

Jess folded her arms across her chest. "This part of the state?"

"Ummm, umm. Jess, I'm a man of science. I have to ... be open to any possibility. There could be, conceivably, a prettier investigator. I doubt it, but it's a possibility."

"Put the shovel down, Jim. You've dug yourself a deep enough hole."

"I suppose you're right," he said, a boyish smile lighting his face.

Jess started closing up files, both virtual and hard copies, on her desk. "Tell me why you really came over to my office."

"Two things." He walked around her desk to stand behind her. "First, to make sure we are still on for dinner tonight."

"Barring all hell breaking loose, absolutely."

His hands slid down from her shoulders to cup each of her breasts, giving them a gentle but deliciously firm squeeze. When he let go, he spun her chair around, and her with it, and pulled her up into his arms.

"Excellent. There's something important I want to talk to you about."

"What is it?"

"Not here." Jim shook his head.

"Then what's the second thing?"

"This."

He brought his lips down on hers. His tongue plunged and probed, leaving a hint of butterscotch candy in its wake.

Her lips tingled as the sensation raced through her body, sending her pulse rate skyrocketing. When he finally broke the kiss, Jess dragged in a ragged breath and gripped Jim's shoulders in order to remain standing.

"That. That was the other thing." Jim took a step away from her, gave his jacket a tug to straighten it, then walked over to her office door. He opened the blinds again. "See you after work, gorgeous."

She watched him leave, gobsmacked, and shook her head in an attempt to clear the fog Jim had created in her brain. *How the hell am I going to focus on police work after that?*

# # #

Suz stepped up to the line, bowling ball in hand, eyeing the pins at the far end of the lane with solid determination. Her side desperately needed her to pick up this spare, the dreaded seven-ten split. In her mind, she imagined the ball sailing down the edge of the lane to hit the seven just right to send it across the empty space into number ten. Drawing in a deep breath, she headed to the foul line, swinging the ball back.

Skidding to a stop just before the line, she sent the ball careening down the oiled lane. As soon as the ball left her fingers, she spun around and covered her eyes. "I can't look. I can't look."

Time slowed down as the entire crowd pulled in a collective breath until a clack split the silence when the ball hit the seven pin followed in a split second by the ten. The entire place broke out in applause. As she uncovered her eyes, her teammates, Jenni and Marianne, jumped and bounced around in celebration.

Wearing a cock-sure smile, she strode over to the guys where they were huddled around the electronic scoring table. "Junior league bowling champ three years straight in high school. I do believe that means you boys owe us pizza."

An hour later, the six of them sat around a table at DaVinci's, devouring three large pizzas and on their second pitcher of soda. They passed around one of the big, silver pizza plates, polishing it off before sending it back to the kitchen.

As he handed off the plate to Colin, Matt pulled something from his jacket pocket. "Marianne, Col. I found a picture a few days ago while emptying out a trunk at the house." He slid the picture in front of Colin, who picked up the photo.

"It's our dads."

"Yeah." Matt nodded. "But who's the girl?"

"Not a clue. She looks about five or six years older." He handed the picture over to his sister. "Any ideas, Marianne?"

Marianne studied the photo. "I agree on the age, Col." She studied it for a moment. "Okay, the dads look like they're eleven, maybe twelve. That would make the girl fifteen, maybe sixteen. But I'd put money on them being related. Some cousin we never met?" She shook her head as she handed the picture back to Matt.

"That's the best I, umm," he looked over at Suz, "*we* could come up with."

A squeeze on her thigh under the table and a flirty wink from Matt cranked Suz's hormones into overdrive. He'd included her in the casual comment, linked them together in front of his closest family.

Maybe he feels the same way I am.

###

The chilly November air sent a shiver through Judge Barnes, causing her to pull her cardigan closed as she entered the living room. Mother had called it the parlor until the day she'd died. The room, empty now of its numerous pieces of antique furniture, needed to be closed up for the winter to save money. Heating oil was getting terribly expensive.

As Madelyn carefully bent down to close the cold air return, something shiny inside the vent caught her eye, virtually obscured by the accumulation of dust and dirt. She lifted the ornate metal grid, exposing the ductwork elbow below the hardwood floor. Teetering down onto her knees, she reached a quivering hand into the opening.

Elbow deep now, her fingertips searched for the object, so curious as to what would have escaped discovery for who knows how long. She brushed across the metal, moving it just out of her reach. Trying again, she finally got it in her grip. *What? A cufflink?*

Lifting it out of the duct, she blew across the cufflink, sending dirt and dust flying into the air. She rubbed her thumb over the piece of masculine jewelry, revealing the engraved monogram.

Judge Barnes gasped then pitched the cufflink across the room, the memories it brought back sending her emotions into a tailspin. "How the..." Her pulse pounded in her chest as if she'd seen a ghost. And in a way she had.

Over fifty years ago, in this very room, the man she'd once thought to marry had drawn his final beaths in agonizing gulps of air. Winslow had dared to threaten her father with exposure, bleeding him dry through blackmail. Men of wealth, presumed or otherwise, including here in the hills of Kentucky, had their vices overlooked—even when they were gambling away what little money the family had left.

Madelyn had slowly, meticulously, exacted her revenge. Cup after dark, sweet cup of coffee Winslow had consumed at the Barnes home had been laced with a syrupy tincture made from foxglove. Everyone in the county knew his father had passed from a heart attack a scant month after Winslow's graduation from the law school in Lexington. When he collapsed there in the living room, not a soul doubted that he'd suffered the same, tragic and untimely death as his father.

"Served him right. Turning against the Barnes family like that." She went to pick up the cufflink again and fidgeted it in her hand, turning it around and around. "Just like those damned MacInneses. They're going to pay, too. Pay dearly."

With the cufflink still clutched in her fist, she slid the pocket doors closed behind her, knowing it would be spring before she opened them up again. Her footsteps echoed down the empty hall, her thoughts swirling as she mulled how she'd exact her revenge on those thieving MacInneses.

They'd stolen her grandfather's bourbon recipe, using it for almost a hundred years now, claiming it as their own. Building their name and filling their coffers with money that should have been her father's, and now her's. She wouldn't be worrying about heating her home, making her own meals. "Or doing my own dirty work."

She wouldn't have admitted it to anyone back then, but exacting her revenge on a pansy-ass like Winslow had given her a thrill like no other. Over the decades, there had been times when she'd taken the reins into her own hands once again. With each instance, her pulse had quickened a bit faster, the satisfaction grown a bit deeper.

The Sheriff would never see it coming.

# # #

"And the shot came out of nowhere?"

Suz nodded at Charlotte's question. "Matt and I had been out on the patio for less than five minutes."

"Do the police have any idea about the shooter?" Charlotte Borden, fiancée of one of Colin's best friends, Hank, was also a journalist in the wine and spirits world.

"Other than where the shooter was and what caliber rifle," Suz blew out a frustrated breath, "they are just as clueless as we are." She took a sip from her glass of tea. "Don't get me wrong, Detective Kent shows up and is doing the work with anything she and her team discover. I have no doubt they're going to get to the bottom of this."

Charlotte jotted down a note. "I'm finally going to talk with her next week. I've heard so much about her from you, Marianne, and

Jenni. I'm convinced this story is going to really rock the entire spirits world."

"I'll be honest with you, I was scared to death when I heard the shot."

Charlotte reached over and squeezed Suz's hand. "I would've been, too. But, it seems to have brought you and Matt together."

Heart fluttering in her chest, Suz smiled. "I've had a kind of crush on him since Marianne introduced me to him back when we were college roommates." She paused for a moment, wondering how much to share. "But things are, well, they're different now."

"Your face just lit up talking about him."

"Let's not make a big deal out of that just yet. Okay? I'm pretty sure Marianne has figured it out, but, you know, just in case..."

"I get it. I was the same way when Hank and I first got together. Didn't want to jinx anything before it really got off the ground."

"Oh, I totally get that. And yeah, I'm feeling the same way."

"Let's get back to the interview," Charlotte interjected. She tapped the resume button on her digital recorder. "So, do you have any theories on the what and why of all these things happening at the MacInnes distillery?"

Suz trailed her fingertip in lazy circles on the tabletop as she tried to put her thoughts into words. "I've got a certain advantage, being both on the inside and the outside of the family. And have been for years."

Charlottes eyes went wide. "I guess I hadn't considered that. Standing on the edge, and yet being able to walk into the inner circle. You can bring a different perspective."

Suz nodded. "I mentioned it to Gray the other day. He's in an even better position. Knowing Colin for several years and only being surrounded by everyone for the past few months."

"And what does your inside-outside perspective suggest to you?"

"I might be totally off base here, but this all feels very personal. MacInnes isn't being targeted just because they're one of the big dogs in distilling. And it isn't from some of the neo-prohibitionists." She shook her head, pushing her hair back from her face. "This is personal. Someone has a big, old axe to grind. And whoever it is, they've decided now's the time."

Chapter 7

The sun hovered just above the crest of the hill, giving the distillery grounds an eerie light as night began to fall. Most of the trees stood dark and bare, with the last dry leaves skittering across the drive.

Suz crept up the ribbon of concrete, past the empty parking lot, and then up the little rise, toward the event center. A chill wind kicked up as she got closer to the building. She crossed into the grass it crunched beneath her shoes.

Tension seeped into her body, radiating up from the ground itself. Only then did she realize that she carried a rifle. A long, heavy rifle. The air around her was eerily quiet, no noise from the distillery or traffic on the road behind her as if she were the only soul around for miles.

Crossing the final few yards, she started up the paved walk when out of the corner of her eye, Suz caught a flicker of movement. She wheeled around, shouldering the weapon.

"Stop where you are!" she shouted.

The man-sized figure turned toward her then halted for only a split second. Suz shuddered as fear gripped her insides. She took a few tentative steps closer to the building, before working the bolt of the rifle to chamber a bullet.

"I'm armed!" she shouted again, louder this time. "I'll shoot. I swear I will."

The person's face was obscured inside a deep hood. Once again, the figure began to move, heading straight toward her. It was still several yards away when she started to back up. Even with her fear, she was unable to tear her gaze from the sight, struck with morbid fascination.

She wasn't going to get away. Not unless she did the unthinkable. She was going to have to shoot. And shoot to kill.

Suz took several steps in rapid succession, steeling her nerves for the inevitable. She shouldered the rifle. Taking careful aim, right at the center of what she imagined was the figure's chest, she squeezed the trigger.

In a split second, the figure collapsed as a voice cried out, "Suz!"

"No!" she screamed as she dropped the gun before taking off in a run. "It ... it can't be."

The figure lay unmoving, sprawled face down on the concrete. A crimson pool spread out at her feet as she knelt. Her fingers shook uncontrollably as she rolled him over and pushed back the hood fabric from his face.

"Matttttttt!" The scream tore out from her throat.

# # #

"Suz? You okay? Come on, wake up, babe."

She shook her head and rubbed her eyes. "Another dream?" Her heart raced.

"Apparently." Matt caressed her bare shoulders. "You started thrashing around, then screamed and sat bolt upright." He slid out of bed. "Hold on. I'll be right back."

Moments later, he held out a glass to her. "Here. Drink. It's the only thing you had in your fridge with sugar in it. Trust me, when that adrenalin wears off, you're gonna crash hard. The sugar will help."

"Thanks." She took a couple of sips of the orange juice, her hands shaking.

"Wanna tell me about it?" Matt slid back into bed beside her before pulling her against him.

After emptying the glass and setting in on the bedside table, Suz nestled onto his shoulder, marveling at just how perfect she fit. Skin to skin. She ran her palm over his chest. "I think I'd better tell you."

Slowly, choosing her words with great care, she told him her dream. Even lying next to him, snuggled in his arms, her stomach knotted as she spun out the final moments of firing the shot.

"I don't have a clue how my imagination conjured you up there at the end. I ... I was so scared, Matt. So scared."

He hugged her tighter. "I'm just glad I got back early so I could be here for you." He kissed the top of her head. "It was a dream, that's all. Our minds don't ask permission about the stories they make up."

Matt flicked out the light on his side of the bed. "Get some rest. We'll talk in the morning."

# # #

Suz swirled the foaming butter around the skillet before she dumped in the whipped eggs. She'd awakened so damned scared last night and having Matt right there, his solid strength wrapping around her, had calmed her jagged nerves. She was starting to get used to falling asleep either with his arm draped over her or his broad back pressed up against hers.

"Morning, sunshine," Matt greeted, his breath warm against her neck. "Happy you were able to get back to sleep last night." He brushed her hair aside and kissed her neck. "I'm not sure what smells better, you or that pot of fresh coffee."

She set the spatula down after giving the eggs a quick stir then swung one of the upper cabinets open. "Take your pick of the mugs. Then get a couple of plates from the next cabinet. These eggs are done."

Once she'd added the bacon from the plate in the oven, they carried their breakfast to the table and sat down.

"Thanks, for umm, you know, last night," she said. "You being here made it easier."

Matt hooked her gaze. "I always want to be here for you." He took another bite, a pensive look on his face. "You might not like this, but I'm going to say it anyway. You need to talk to someone about these dreams."

Fearing she knew where his statement was heading, she feigned misunderstanding. "I've got Marianne and you. Heck, even Jenni and now Charlotte."

He all but rolled his eyes. "You know what I mean. A therapist or something."

She nodded. "I will, if these dreams continue."

Matt covered her hand with his work-roughened one. "How much worse do you want them to get? Get real. Do you want to fight one of them every night?"

"No." The idea of the dreams getting worse and more frequent chilled her to her very soul.

"That's the risk you take if you don't deal with this. Trust me, I know."

Leaning over, Suz hugged him. "I don't want to take away from what you've gone through."

"As much as I like your hugs, I'm focusing on you this morning." He picked up his coffee mug and took a drink. "I can help you find a good therapist. There's even one or two good online services you could get hooked up with."

"Seriously? You don't think its wimpy?" She poked and prodded her scrambles with the fork. "Despite dad's academia reputation, my folks didn't hold much with, as Dad puts it, *psychobabble.*" She made air quotes with her fingers.

"No worries. They won't hear about it from me." Matt shoved a forkful of food into his mouth and swallowed. "Hell no, it's definitely not wimpy. I still go on occasion. I imagine Colin does too but I've never asked, and he's never mentioned it . Grey too, most likely. He was in that helo when it went down along with Col."

"Umm, I never looked at it that way. Guess it wouldn't be too bad to make a visit or two."

Matt grinned at her as if he saw through her charade. "My day isn't going to be too long today. That batch of staves is supposed to arrive before lunch, so I'll spend a couple of hours sorting and stacking. How about you?"

"Meeting with a new client at ten for a wedding in the spring." She rolled her eyes. "The bride and her mother. I am not looking forward to this."

"Glad it's you, not me." Using his toast as a pusher, he scooped up the final bit of eggs and followed that with the bread and bacon. "Wanna go out for beer and pizza this evening?"

"I'd love to. What time and where?"

# # #

Suz took a sip of her iced tea. The meeting with that bride-to-be and her mother had gone so much better than anticipated. Even though the things the younger woman wanted were on the extravagant side, the budget Suz had been given would definitely handle the event. Not to mention that the bride's mother hadn't tried to force her own opinions on her daughter.

While this was going to take a lot of work and planning, the event would expose her business to a wider social circle for gigs. Things had picked up since the event at the MacInnes distillery—she'd already gotten three bookings from the pocket full of business cards she'd brought home.

While her business life was running smooth on solid ground, her personal life had her on her toes. Matthew MacInnes made her heart, and parts farther south, race with desire. He ticked all of her boxes. *Doesn't he?*

She crossed her fingers, hopeful that she wasn't seeing him through those rose-colored glasses she'd been accused of in the past. Men—no, boys, now that she looked back, that her parents had encouraged her to date. Oh, they'd been pleasant enough, smart enough, sexy enough. But she'd always found them to be missing something. And now she knew what that something had been.

Work. Real, honest, sweaty, dirty work. Something the entire MacInnes family knew firsthand. She'd heard the story of how everyone had pitched in to clean up the trashed bottling room. Had seen Colin, with the elder MacInnes brothers, shirt sleeves rolled up helping roll barrels when a particularly wicked gut flu had over half of the warehousemen home sick.

But to her mind, none of them knew that work more than Matt. While Marianne fussed over what she considered *her* bourbon, Suz knew that he considered each and every resting barrel his, even though he hadn't personally built them. He looked over every semi load that came into the distillery, walked the warehouses checking for barrels that were leaking or needed repair.

Many of the ladies who worked at MacInnes cast admiring looks through the open doors of the cooperage, watching Matt at work, especially on hot summer days. She'd done it herself, more times than she wanted to admit. Days when he was working steel into hoops or charring barrels, she'd found him shirtless, skin slick and muscles tight.

"Stop that," she said out loud.

Once she had the estimate drafted, Suz hit save and closed the computer file. She'd double check the math and current pricing from one of her favorite vendors tomorrow before emailing the proposal to the bride and her family.

After she'd locked her office door, she waved at Francine, the fortyish accountant who rented the one across the hall. "See ya Monday."

The woman looked up, smiled, and waved back. "If I ever get this mess straightened out."

"Don't stay too late."

Once outside, Suz walked across the parking lot to her SUV. It looked bigger than it really was, sitting there surrounded by the more economical cars driven by the other building tenants. "At least you're easy to find." She patted the hood.

It was then that she noticed the envelope stuffed under the wiper blade. Puzzled, she tugged it free. Fliers promoting local events often got circulated this way, but she'd never found anything like this. Just a plain white envelope, her name scrawled on the front looking like it had been written by a child.

She ripped it open. Inside was a single sheet of paper, folded neatly into thirds. Her hand started to shake as she read the message: *If you know what's good for you, stay away from the MacInnes family.*

# # #

"You're not going to do that, are you?"

"Do what?" She took a big bite of pizza.

Matt tapped a finger against the paper on the table. "Stay away from me. I mean us." He reached across the table, covering her hand in his.

Suz swallowed then shook her head. "I'm not a fraidy cat. Nope, you're stuck with me." "Any idea who left this for you?" The timbre of his voice took on a hint of a growl. Low, deep and almost feral. "Have you told Detective Kent about it yet?"

His face visibly relaxed before lighting up in a smile. "You had me worried for a minute there." He lifted her hand from the table and planted a sweet little kiss in her palm. "Now that's settled, I have to ask you something more important. What are you doing for Thanksgiving?"

"Ummm, I'm not sure. My father is speaking at a conference and they won't be back until the weekend after. So I'm going to dinner the on the Sunday after—"

"Great, then you can come to ours with me. If you want to, that is."

In that brief instant, seeing the excited little boy inside the man across the table, Suz knew, beyond a shadow of a doubt, that she was done for.

"I'd absolutely love to spend Thanksgiving with you and your family."

# # #

Matt dropped her onto the big bed, naked but for her tiny thong. "Those will have to go, too, you know." He tugged them down past her knees and tossed them onto the floor. "Much better."

"You said something about devouring me. Dessert, I believe you called it after carrying me up the stairs, fireman style."

He ran his tongue over his lips. "Ah, yes." Grabbing her ankles, he spread them wide before settling in between them. "So pretty," he moaned, stroking her with first one finger and then two as he rocked back onto his heels.

The sensation he created with the scissoring motion brushing past her clit drove her wild. She bucked, arching up to him, causing his fingers to slip just barely inside.

"More, please," she begged.

"As you wish." He stretched out on his stomach between her thighs, then parted her folds with both thumbs.

She loved being spread wide for Matt. His tongue stroking her pussy, tasting her. Kissing her with her wetness on his lips. "Oh yes, please..."

His tongue and lips settled on her clit, sucking it, swirling his tongue around it. "Delicious," he growled as he pushed two fingers inside her.

Unable to keep still, Suz writhed and squirmed as her thighs began to quiver. "If . . . if you don't stop . . . now, and give me that cock . . . I ..."

He laughed against her wetness. "Or you'll what, my darling?"

"I'll come ... without ... you," she finally managed to gasp out.

"Ah, ah, ah, not until I say so." Matt pulled his fingers out, making a show of licking her juices from them. Then he repositioned himself to put the tip of his cock at her entrance, hooking his arms under her knees.

She instinctively arched against him as he thrust in deep, stretching and filling her so perfectly. She matched his rhythm, stroke for hard, deep stroke, fighting the urge to let go.

Suz gripped his shoulders, feeling the taut muscles bunch and relax under his skin. "Please," she begged. "I can't hold back any longer."

"Yes," he groaned. "Now, sweetheart. *Now*."

Having all the encouragement she needed, Suz released her control.

# # #

Matt slid into bed after turning out the bathroom light. The satisfied, female moan from the next pillow was something he hadn't heard in years. There'd been lovers in the past, sure. But those had been the enjoy-and-head-home type, not a spend-the-night, snuggled-up-next-to type, like the woman currently teetering at the edge of sleep beside him.

"Sleep well, gorgeous." He nibbled and kissed across her bare shoulder.

Her eyes fluttered, half opening. "Night, Matt. You, too." She lifted her head off the pillow just long enough to kiss him back when he claimed her lips.

His vision had adjusted to the darkness of the bedroom so he enjoyed studying her as she fell into a well-deserved slumber. Smart, sweet, and oh so sexy. *What did I do to earn this woman?*

He'd already begun to admit that he had fallen for Suz, but he thought it too early to share his feelings with her. *Soon, though.* Now that he had her interested, he wasn't about to let her go. This was not going to be a catch and release relationship.

Matt settled down under the covers and snuggled against that wonderfully curvy ass. Definitely an ass man, he'd made an intense study of the female backside since he was a teenager. As far as he was concerned, Suz Benton had the absolute best ass ever.

Yep, the absolute best.

#

"You did what?" Madelyn Barnes snapped over the telephone line.

"I sent a warning letter to that girl the barrel maker MacInnes has been seeing."

"Did I tell you to do that? Did I, Sheriff?" She shook her head, knowing he'd just absolutely sealed his fate.

"No. But I saw the look on her face. She's spooked, just like the other MacInnes cousin. The one that's going to be the next master distiller."

"No, no, she won't. By the time I'm finished with that blasted family, there'll be nothing left of the MacInnes Distillery or their bourbon. Nothing but a memory." Anger rose in her chest as she thumped her fist against the desk. "Nothing!"

There'd be a purple bruise there tomorrow, but Madelyn didn't care. She'd go to any lengths to destroy that thieving family.

"Now that I think on it, you may have done me a favor, Sheriff."

"I did?"

She heard the relief in his voice and shook her head. He was a pathetic sort of man at the core of it. So easily manipulated. "Yes, I do believe you did. Tell me, could you get me a few of those road flares you and your deputies use?"

"Of course. How many?"

The plan started to solidify in her mind. "Not many. Four or five. Whatever you can get for me."

"No problem at all. How soon do you want them?"

How soon indeed? This idea was going to take a bit of planning. But it had to be ready for when opportunity struck. "Bring them to the campaign dinner next week." After that night, there'd be no one who knew she had the flares.

"Yes, Ma'am. I can do that."

"Good. Then we can forget that little faux pas of yours ever happened."

"Thank you, Judge. By the way, would you like a lift to the dinner?"

His voice quivered the tiniest bit. *Good.* Her years on the bench had shown how pliable people could be when afraid. "Think no more of it, water under the bridge. Just make sure you bring those flares."

"I won't forget. And Judge, thanks again for another endorsement."

"My pleasure. Now, run along. I have things I need to get done."

Chapter 8

Suz stirred her straw in circles through the whipped cream atop the hot café mocha. "How'd you know?"

Marianne broke off one corner of her cranberry scone. "Know what?" She popped the morsel into her mouth.

"That Gray is the right guy."

"Falling for Matt, are we?" Marianne grinned. "Sorry, it's just nice to hear you're finally admitting it."

"Stop gloating." Suz took a sip of the steamy drink. "Yeah, I think he might be my Mister Right."

"All right. All kidding aside, I'm going to assume you're enjoying the time you spend with him. And that he totally rocks your boat in the bedroom."

"Duh." Suz hoped the flush that crept up from her core didn't show on her face. "Yes to both of those assumptions."

"Where do you see your life in the next five or ten years?"

Her friend's question pulled Suz up short. What did she want? "I want my business to grow, obviously."

"So, close your eyes. Imagine coming home from some event you planned. What do you want to see?"

What did she want? A home? A husband? Kids? "Umm, I, I..."

"Come on. Work with me here." Marianne took a drink of her coffee. "Can you see your future without Matt in it?"

Before she realized what she was saying, Suz blurted out, "No."

# # #

"It's open," Suz called out when she heard Matt's knock at the door.

Less than a moment later, he walked into her kitchen. "Oh gawd, what smells so good?"

"Dinner."

"I figured, since you invited me over for that very thing." He leaned over her shoulder and pulled in a deep breath.

"Since it was cold and rainy today, and I felt like Italian. This," she dipped a spoon into the pot and offered him a taste, "is my take on pasta e fagioli soup."

"Delish. And what's in the oven."

"Garlic bread, what else?" She turned the flame down as low as she could. "Grab the wine and glasses and I'll get the salads."

After several moments of dinner and small talk, Matt got up and walked over to where his leather jacket lay draped over the sofa. After fiddling with it, he came back to his seat.

"I got you something."

"What is it?" She dabbed at her lips, her curiosity piqued.

"Just something I thought you needed to have." He held out one hand, closed around something small.

"Let me see."

He dropped it into her hand, the metal warm from his body heat. The second she realized what it was, she gasped, almost dropping it into her bowl.

She stared at the object: on a simple keyring, just one lonely key. "What's this?"

"A key to my house. I want you to be able to go in even if I'm not home."

Her hands started shaking. "Seriously? You want me to have this?"

Matt nodded. "Yes. I think our relationship is going places. Places that kinda scare me. But I want us to be scared together."

She laid the key down next to her glass and gave her head a little shake, then smiled. "You're not going to believe this."

Suz got up and walked into the living room. From the candy dish on the coffee table, she picked up the item she'd gotten for him and went back to the dining room, standing next to him. "I was going to wait until later, but..." She dangled it from her fingers.

"Is this what I think it is?" Matt asked.

"Yup, unlocks that door right over there." She pointed to her own front door. "If you ever need to get in when I have another nightmare, you can. But now, I think that ship has sailed. It's more than that."

Still in his chair, Matt looked up at her. "Thank you."

She wrapped her arms around his neck and laced her fingers together. "Why?"

"For trusting me to be the one who shows up when your nightmares happen."

# # #

"Matt, ya got a few minutes?"

Looking up from his work, Matt saw Colin standing at the cooperage door. "Give me a minute." The stopwatch in his hand ticked off the seconds as he waited for the flames inside the barrel to do their magic. Finally, it reached the target. With moves that relied mostly on muscle memory, he took the barrel off the burner without getting burned himself, then sprayed the inside using the garden hose.

As the smoke and steam billowed out, he moved the barrel over to a safe spot in the shop. "Thanks for waiting. Marianne asked for this char special for one of her experimental batches."

"Not a problem. She's doing great work for the brand. No wonder Uncle Wes had been turning more of the major decisions over to her."

"You should hear Dad brag on her. I know he's not going to completely retire for quite some time, but my money's on Marianne getting the assistant knocked off her title before he hits sixty. He and Mom want to do some travelling."

"I've heard my dad say that, too. Scotland and Ireland are high on the list."

"Yeah." Matt peered into the barrel. "She's looking for a level three."

Colin tipped the barrel in his direction. "You nailed it."

Matt rubbed his fingernails on his chest. "Was there ever a doubt?"

The cousins shared a laugh over their shared MacInnes cockiness. "Now that we got that taken care of, what can I do for you?"

"We're gonna announce it next week at the family Thanksgiving dinner. But I want you to hear it from me first."

Matt gave his cousin a side eye glance. "You saying what I think you're saying?"

"Maybe."

"So, spill it."

"Jenni and I are are gonna get married."

"Hot damn." Matt walked over and smacked Colin on the back then pulled him into a hug. "Congrats, man. I'm thrilled for you. Jenni's a great lady."

"Glad you feel that way, Matt, 'cause I need to ask you something."

"Go for it." Matt leaned back against the tool bench, arms crossed over his chest.

"Be my best man."

He swallowed hard, trying to keep from tearing up. "You don't have to feel obligated 'cause we're cousins ya know."

"We've been each other's wing man since we had training wheels on our bikes. There's no one else I'd rather have stand up with me."

"Man, I'd be honored." He grabbed Colin's hand and shook it, sealing the deal. "Now I wish I'd kept a bottle down here."

"Got one in my office."

"Let me shut things off and lock up, and I'll be right there."

"It'll go quicker if we both do it."

# # #

Judge Barnes reached behind her neck to fasten the clasp on her grandmother's pearls, the only piece remaining from her inheritance. All of the other pieces had been sold off over the years, along with the antique furniture, to make ends meet. All the more reason to carry on with her plans.

But tonight, she needed to get rid of the only remaining link between herself and the recent troubles that had befallen the MacInnes clan. Sheriff David Whitaker.

She gathered up her purse and wrap—these November nights were getting colder here in central Kentucky. Once the car was idling to warm up, she tucked both her cane and that blasted walker, left over from when she'd fallen and severely wrenched her left knee, in the trunk. No one would think twice about a woman her age using either one.

Acting a bit feebler than she actually was, Judge Madelyn Barnes let herself teeter a bit on her cane as she walked up to the knot of Sheriff Whitaker's loyal supporters. "Folks, I'm so sorry to interrupt. Sheriff, may I have a word with you?"

"Of course, Judge Barnes," he said.

She stepped off to one side as he made his polite excuses to the circle of supporters then joined her. "Would you go out to my car and get the walker out of the trunk?" She added a sly wink so he'd understand. "I'm afraid I'm not as steady on my feet tonight as I should be."

For a split second he seemed not to comprehend, but then the light of understanding dawned. "I'd be happy to, Judge. And while I'm at it, I'll put the package of cookies my mother sent for you inside the vehicle."

"That would be lovely. Please thank her for me. I'll just go sit down at my spot and wait for you there."

She handed her car keys to Whitaker and watched him head off to the parking lot. At least he had the presence of mind to make up that bit about the cookies.

As quiet and unassuming as she could manage, she made her way over to the chair assigned to her at the head table. Madelyn had used her influence to arrange for her to be seated right beside Sheriff Whitaker.

From inside her floral handkerchief, she managed to sprinkle a powder made from her foxglove leaves onto the green salad sitting beside his plate. She saved a bit in hopes she might be able to also get some on his steak later. The syrup she'd dosed full of foxglove tincture would have to wait until their server had filled their iced tea glasses.

That should do it. By morning, the county should be waking up to the news of Sheriff Whitaker's untimely death.

"Here you go, Judge."

She turned around to find the sheriff unfolding the frame of her walker right behind her chair. "Oh, yes, thank you, Dave." Lord, but she hated that thing, and everything it embodied.

"No problem at all, Judge. Here's your keys." He set them beside her plate.

Scooping them up, she dropped them into her small purse. "Looks like they're about to get started."

The venue staff started began the meal plates and filling drink glasses. During the dinner, Judge Barnes managed to dose Whitaker's sweet tea. Even with other opportunities, she feared adding any more of the foxglove, aware of the risk that might present.

The MC settled down the crowd. Once everyone had quieted, he proceeded to the greetings and hinted at the announcement to come. "Now, ladies and gents, I'd like to invite to the podium one of the best loved judges to ever sit the bench here in the Commonwealth. Please join me in a round of heartfelt applause for Judge Madelyn Barnes."

She rose from her chair and made her way to the podium, using her cane. "Thank you, Thomas." The applause slowly died down. "Please. Please, folks, you are much too kind. In the past two elections for sheriff here in Franklin County, I have had the great honor to endorse Sheriff Dave Whitaker. It will come to no one's surprise that I am once again giving my endorsement to his third bid for election."

The crowd exploded into thunderous applause. As she looked around, the sheriff was busily gulping down the last of his second glass of iced tea. She'd surreptitiously managed to dose his second glass, too, though with not as much as the first one. She had no desire for him to fall over while giving his candidacy speech.

Once he arrived at the podium, he draped one arm around her shoulders. "Thank you, Judge Barnes. The folks of Kentucky have always counted on you to be an example of what is right and good here in the Commonwealth. Your years on the bench are a testament to fair and consistent justice. I am immensely proud to once again earn your support and endorsement."

Whitaker turned to his campaign manager. "Steve, would you escort the judge back to her chair, please? I've a few prepared remarks before our fine kitchen staff serve dessert."

Madelyn watched him for signs rather than listened to his speech. As he finished up, she could tell he was already beginning to show the effects. Once dessert was served, she feigned fatigue, and then made her goodbyes.

Once she was back at home, she carried the bag of road flares into the house. She tucked the plain brown paper bag into the bottom desk drawer, giving it a little pat before locking it away. Tomorrow, she'd finalize her plans. One never knew when the opportunity was going to strike. But Madelyn Barnes would be ready.

# # #

"Dispatch, this is unit thirty-five. Over."

"Unit thirty-five, this is dispatch. What've you got?"

"Dispatch, we're responding to a bystander call of a car hitting the bridge over the river on route six-seven-six. Can confirm a single vehicle accident, on the north end of the bridge. Single, male occupant is the restrained driver."

"Unit thirty-five, do you require EMS to the scene?"

There was a prolonged pause before the deputy responded, "Negative dispatch. Requesting response by tow and coroner. Driver is

DOA upon my arrival on scene." The deputy sniffled before adding, "Sherryl, it's the sheriff. He's dead."

# # #

Jess Kent knocked on the office door frame. "Got anything for me?"

Looking up from the report on his desk, Jim said, "Don't leave me an opening like that."

She cocked her head to one side. "We can discuss that later this evening." She walked inside, closing the door behind her. "Tell me you've got the autopsy on Sheriff Whitaker."

"I pulled rank and I'm not letting anyone else be primary."

"Good." She perched herself on the corner of his desk. "So, I know it's not done, but what ya got so far?"

"Tox and stomach contents analysis aren't back yet. We know he's got a cardiac history so an MI isn't out of question."

"Speak English."

"Heart attack. MI stands for myocardial infarction. Thought you knew that." He went to stand in front of her and slid his hand up her calf, over her knee and farther up.

Jess caught his hand through her skirt when it was halfway up her thigh. "Stop that, I need to keep a clear head. I've got everyone, from my chief, to the mayor, to the governor on my ass. I need to get cause of death chop-chop. Natural causes or did someone help him over to the other side?"

"You'll know as soon as I do." He pulled his hand out from under the fabric. "Seems he wrecked the car on his way home from the banquet, but that didn't cause his death. He was gone before he hit that bridge."

Jim slid a hand around her neck, pulling her face to his, kissing her hard and deep before letting go. "You still coming over tonight?"

Jess nodded. "Unless something happens to bust this whole case open. This is tied to the whole MacInnes thing. I just know it."

# # #

"Slow down, Matt."

He stopped and looked back over one shoulder. "Come on, Suz. I don't want to let the food get soaking wet in this rain." He lifted the box he was carrying just a bit higher to emphasize his words.

"I'm nervous." Suz hustled to catch up.

"What are you nervous about? You've known my family for years."

"Yeah, as Marianne's friend. But it's different now."

He gave her a look of complete confusion. "I don't get it."

"I don't expect you to." She fought back the urge to roll her eyes at him. "I'm dating you now. The whole family, especially your folks, are going to look at me different."

He jostled the box to hold it with one arm. With the other, he pulled her tight against him. Without warning, he claimed her mouth in a firm kiss.

Their embrace got interrupted by a booming masculine voice from the porch. "Matthew, let the girl go so she can get in out of the rain."

As they pulled apart, Suz felt the flush of heat that was likely coloring her face. "Your dad. He saw you kissing me."

Matt laughed. "Well, if they didn't know before, they sure do now."

"Is he going to tell the whole family?"

She headed up the step to the porch and shook her jacket, sending a shower of water onto the porch.

"He's not gonna broadcast it, but..." He, too, gave his coat a shake, then held the door open for her.

At least she knew everyone in the room. She gave his parents gentle hugs. Gloria, his mom, gave her a knowing smile. "Glad you're here, dear."

Thanksgiving with the whole MacInnes clan had always been a rowdy and boisterous affair, at least the times Suz had been present. And this year looked like no exception. The old two-car garage had been converted into a family room years ago. The sofa, armchairs, and recliners had been rearranged around the big screen television.

Matt had already settled in next to Marianne, who was sitting in the middle of the sofa, with Gray on her other side. "What's the score?" he asked to no one in particular.

"Seven-zip, UK. Two minutes left in the first quarter," Colin replied.

Matt's mom leaned in to softly ask, "Big football fan?"

Suz shook her head. "No more than I have to be. Basketball's more my style."

"Wait till the season really gets going around here. Things get so noisy you can barely hear yourself think." She gripped Suz's elbow. "Come on into the kitchen. Jenni's in there with Sallie. We've got wine and cheese, and it's much more civilized."

Suz followed Matt's mom through the dining room and into the big farm-style kitchen. Jenni was filling a new wine glass, which she handed off as Suz walked in.

"Oh, this is yummy." Suz took a second sip. "A gewürztraminer?"

Jenni nodded. "Gray's suggestion. Says it goes well with roast turkey."

"I think he might be on to something here." Suz took another sip. "Oh, I could get used to this."

"I know, right?" Jenni giggled. "Here," she handed Suz a cracker with some sort of creamy, cheesy looking spread on it, "try this."

She popped the morsel into her mouth and the flavors exploded. "What?" She smacked her lips, trying to make them out. "Shallot. Something sweet, umm, apple? No, it's honey."

"Keep going, you're on a roll," Gloria said as she carried a pot to the sink. "I need to drain the potatoes."

"There's more than one cheese, isn't there?"

"Yup," Jenni spread some of it on a piece of celery.

Before Suz could continue guessing the ingredients, Marianne poked her head in the door. "The guys want to know how long before dinner."

"I'm shooting for half time," Gloria replied. "Has the second quarter started?"

Marianne nodded. "Just did."

Gloria set the pot of boiled potatoes down and then checked her watch. "Yeah, we're good. Should be just perfect. Tell them dinner's at half time."

Before leaving, Marianne scooped up a cracker with the mysterious cheese dip on it. "Oh, so that's what Gray decided to make. Fig and stilton spread." She popped it into her mouth, quickly chewed and swallowed. "Damn, he's good."

The four of them stared behind her as the kitchen door swung on its hinges.

"Figs, huh?" Gloria put the lid on the potato pot.

"Evidently. Guess that's the reason she's the distiller." Suz grabbed up another cracker and quickly devoured it.

"Sallie, would you and Jenni take the plates and silverware out to the sideboard where I thought we'd put the food out buffet style this year?"

Suz noted the knowing looks shared between the two mothers and her gut tightened. She knew what was coming, and silently braced herself.

"You look like you're expecting a butt-chewing."

Suz bit her lip in nervous dread. "Kinda."

"Well, stop that." Gloria opened the refrigerator door and took out a new box of butter. "I only wanted a few minutes to let you know how pleased I am that my hard-headed son has finally wised up and realized there's been a damned good woman right in front of his eyes for years."

"Oh, umm, I'm glad you think so." *Is the other shoe about to drop?*

"Relax, dear." Gloria hugged her. "In this, I'm on your side."

Suz's tension melted away at last. "I admit. I was sort of worried about coming to the family Thanksgiving dinner today."

"You put that out of your mind right now, hon. Wes and I both hope everything works out for you two."

Breathing a deep sigh of relief, Suz returned the older woman's hug. "Thanks."

"Let's get this dinner finished and ready to go on the table. Put those rolls in the oven to heat up while I mash the potatoes."

# # #

"You knew and didn't say anything?"

Matt shrugged as he walked out of the bathroom. "Col asked me to keep it quiet till the dinner today."

She walked over and hugged his bare torso. "What do you think about them getting married? I mean, she ditched him once."

"Marianne and I were both worried about them getting back together. The parents, too." He pulled her closer, his hands cupping her backside and squeezing. "But she's changed. I don't know if you remember, but she was a huge party girl back then. Something happened while they were split up. Colin won't say anymore, only that it's not his story to tell."

"That's a good thing, I guess." She gave him a quick kiss before slipping out of their hug and giving him a playful smack on the ass. For a split second, she considered telling him about the conversation she'd had with his mother, but then changed her mind. No, that was a special little moment she'd just keep to herself.

"Feeling playful, are you?" Matt cocked one brow, giving her one of his you'd-better-mean-business looks.

"You betcha."

"Strip. And get that sweet ass in bed."

A wide and wicked smile lit her face. "Yes, sir."

Chapter 9

The knock on the doorframe pulled Jess from the report she was reading. "From the look on your face, Terri, you've got something unusual for me."

"You could say that." The woman many considered to be the best ballistics tech in the state walked onto Jess' office, closing the door behind her. "I've got a match for one of your open cases."

"Which?"

Terri laid the report printout on the desk. "The MacInnes shooting."

"I thought you told me we didn't have a match." Jess picked up the form and began to scan through the boxes filled with data. "What the...? Is this right?"

Terri nodded. "I ran it myself. Three times, just to make sure. The gun used to make the shot out at MacInnes was, at least in theory, in custody, locked in the evidence room."

"But how?" Jess asked, already fearing she knew the answer.

"That's up to you to figure out. But seems to me you've got a dirty cop on your hands."

"I want that rifle moved—"

Terri stood up from her chair. "Already in the works. It's being dusted for prints and examined for trace as we speak."

"Thank you. I figured you had something important for me, but I never expected to have evidence of a dirty cop."

"Sorry. In times like this, I'm glad I went to the technical side, rather than the investigative side of our work." Terri headed back to the door. "Let me know if you need anything else."

For several minutes after Terri left, Jess just stared at the report. The rifle had been confiscated from the truck owned by a young punk who'd held up a convenience store. He hadn't even used the long gun in the robbery, which was why the ballistics had been delayed.

In the quiet of her office, the phone rang, startling Jess out of her thoughts. "Kent."

"Hello, Jess."

"Jim." Her pulse always fluttered a bit when she talked to him. More than it possibly should given their simple friends with benefits relationship.

"I've got the Whitaker autopsy results and lab reports for you. You'll get the full reports in hard copy, but you need to hear this today."

She grabbed a notepad and pen, unable to fight the suspicion that this was going to complicate the case even further. "I'm ready. Give it to me."

"My suspicion was right. He was dead before the car hit the bridge abutment. Sudden cardiac arrest. His potassium level was way off."

"So, no foul play. Natural causes." Jess put her pen down.

"Not so fast. Analysis of the stomach contents, however, revealed the cause."

"Well, don't keep me in suspense. What caused his cardiac arrest?"

"Foxglove. Or more specifically, digitalis. A drug used to treat heart failure." He paused before continuing, "According to the information I have from his primary physician, Sheriff Whitaker did not have heart failure, just simple high blood pressure. He wasn't taking anything that contained digitalis."

"He was poisoned."

"That's what's going in as cause of death. Cardiac arrest due to digitalis poisoning."

"He was murdered." She wrote a big M on the notepad. "I knew it. I knew it." She shared the information about the ballistics with him. "I'm beginning to think our sheriff might have been the dirty cop."

"Then, given that he was likely poisoned, that suggests to me that someone is trying to tie up loose ends," Jim added.

Oscar. Her thoughts trailed back to that evening back in the summer. How convenient that Sheriff Whitaker just happened to be there when the MacInnes maintenance man had swerved off of the road. "Jim, I gotta go. I need to get a warrant."

I# # #

"Thank you, folks, for coming."

"I must admit, Detective, I'm confused as to why you called us together for this." Colin leaned back against his desk.

"I normally wouldn't. But in this case, there are extenuating circumstances."

"What circumstances?" Matt draped a protective arm over Suz's shoulder, while both Gray and Colin made similar moves.

Matt hadn't been able to shake the sense of foreboding ever since he and Suz had walked into Colin's office this morning. The serious look on the detective's face only served to intensify the air of uncertainty.

"I'm certain you've all heard that Sheriff Whitaker died the other evening."

Heads nodded around the room.

"What does that have to do with the incidents going on around here?" Marianne asked.

"What I'm about to say is confidential. We have reason to believe that he was murdered. When we searched his home and belongings, we found a second car. A car that contained explosives and wiring that matches the device used to explode that vehicle your maintenance man Oscar was driving the night he was killed."

Gray shifted on his feet. "With the Sheriff dead, does this mean your investigation is closed?"

Jess shook her head. "We now have a ballistics match from the shooting that happened during the event center party."

Matt's gut tightened. "You've identified the shooter?" He fought back the urge to demand a name.

The detective shook her head. "The gun used to fire the shot was in police custody at the time of the shooting. Supposedly locked inside our evidence room."

"That means there's a dirty cop," Suz added, her tone barely above a whisper. "And if it was the sheriff..."

"Someone is cleaning up loose ends," Matt finished her sentence.

Kent nodded. "That's about the size of it. And it's the reason I wanted all six of you here. Suz got the threatening note, but you're all involved. Please, take extra precautions. If possible, don't go anywhere alone, especially here on the distillery grounds. Ladies, this is not the time for bravado. Stay extra alert until all this gets sorted out."

Uncomfortable silence hung in the air until Colin voiced what all of them were likely thinking. "Thank you for the information and the warning, Detective Kent. We'll let you know if anything out of the ordinary happens."

Jess made sure each of them had her contact information. "Day or night, I don't care, call me. I want this S.O.B." She then gathered her things and headed to the office door, pausing right before walking out. Her hand on the door knob and without looking back, she added, "I didn't say this and you never heard it. If I were y'all, I wouldn't leave the house unarmed."

# # #

"Wow, she's spooked," Jenni broke the silence after the detective's departure.

Matt shook his head. "I'd say more angry and frustrated. She's been working this case since the spring. Every break she gets, it just keeps getting deeper."

"But she's right. I think we're finally coming up against whoever has been the brains behind this whole thing," Colin pointed out.

Marianne stood and began to pace around the office like a caged cat. "I, for one, am going to take her advice about carrying." She looked over at Gray. "And don't even think about locking me up in my office again."

Suz shrugged out from under Matt's arm and inched up to sit on the edge of the sofa. "I agree with Marianne. I'm not going to hide either. I'll be careful, but I will not cower."

"Me neither," Jenni agreed.

"At least Marianne's here where we can keep an eye on her." Matt had to say something about Suz's safety. "Suz is out there running back and forth between Louisville and Lexington virtually every day of the week. I gotta admit, I'm not feeling too good about that."

"I'm with ya there, Matt. At least Jenni's inside the KDA office building," Colin added.

"All I need is my phone, laptop, and access to the internet. How about you, Jenni? Will the KDA let you work remote?" Suz asked.

"I'm sure I can work out something."

Suz's mind swirled with possibilities. "How about this? Colin, you got an empty office or something with room for a couple of desks or tables?"

He nodded. "I think we can make this work."

# # #

Suz looked in her rearview mirror, watching Matt pull into the slot next to her. Exiting her SUV, she walked around to his door. "Thanks for following me home, Matt."

He unfastened his seatbelt and slowly opened the door on the Bug. "You don't get it. You're going in there, packing a suitcase, and getting what you need for work. You're coming home with me till this is over."

"And you were going to tell me when?"

"I thought you had already figured it out." Matt got out of the car and faced her. "Besides, we've been sleeping together more than half the time, anyway."

"It's not the sleeping together that I'm po'd about."

"Then what is it, babe?"

"Control." She turned, heading to her door. Once they were both inside, she turned to face him. "You didn't even talk to me about it. "

"You really hadn't figured it out. You gir...umm, ladies didn't talk?"

"Who had time? Anyway, Jenni already lives with Colin. Gray practically has had Marianne under house arrest since summer." Leaving her purse on the sofa, Suz hung up her jacket before handing a hanger to Matt. "Here."

"We're not really gonna be here that long." Matt pulled his off and draped it over the back of one of the chairs. "Grab what you need for at least two or three days. Like I said, you're coming home with me." He crossed the room to her. "Look, Suz. I do not want to start a fight with you." He trailed a fingertip down the side of her face. "What I do want to do is keep you safe."

"Oh, Matthew." She thumped one loose fist against his chest. "I don't want to argue either. And if I'm going to have to stay with you..." She rested her forehead over his heart. "Yes, I get the safety issue. I don't want us fighting, not while cooped up in the same house."

Matt raked his fingers through her hair. "Me neither." He quietly held her for a few brief moments. "Then grab your stuff. 'Cause if we stand here like this for much longer, I'm going to drag you to your bedroom."

Before lifting her face up, Suz smiled where he couldn't see. "And do what?" she asked, feigning innocence.

A deep, primal growl escaped his lips. "You know damned well. I'd bend you over the bed, pull those jeans down over that delectable ass, then fuck you hard and deep."

Her chest tightened as erotic sensations zinged right to her clit, wetness pooling between her thighs. "What's stopping you?"

"I don't have anything in my wallet."

She suppressed a giggle. "I do. Drawer in my bedside table. Though, I admit, they might be outdated. I've had a bit of a," Suz gave him what she hoped was a thoroughly wicked wink, "dry spell until recently."

"Not gonna chance it, sweetheart." He gave her ass a playful smack. "Get this butt in gear. I want you. In my house. On my bed."

# # #

The whole ride back to his house, Matt kept a hand on her thigh, moving it only to shift gears. Once they were inside, her stuff ended up in a pile right inside by the front door. She started to bound up the stairs when he caught her by the belt loops and tugged. "What the...?"

"Slow down. We've got all night."

Her brow furrowed. "What happened to bent over? Hard and deep?"

"Oh, it's already hard." He placed her hand over the fly of his jeans.

The rock-hard ridge of his erection twitched against her palm. "So I see."

"And it's going to be very deep." He stroked two fingers over her lips.

She poked her tongue out, licking his digits, then parted her lips, wordlessly inviting them to enter. She sucked on them then, gentle at first, in and out, licking and tasting his skin.

He groaned, low and deep in his chest. "Dear gawd, yes, sweetheart." Matt pulled his fingers from her mouth and wiped them against his jeans, then took her hand in his. "Now we're going upstairs."

Right outside his bedroom, he pinned her against the door, cuffing her wrists up over her head with one hand. And with the other, he cupped the side of her face before claiming her lips again.

Their tongues dueled back and forth, taunting, teasing, and exploring. Soon, she was arching her hips against his. Heat and desire pushed all thoughts out of her mind other than the delicious fire between them.

She managed to pull her lips away from his. "Take me to bed, please"

"That is definitely my plan, sweetheart." He tugged and pulled, freeing her blouse from the waistband of her jeans. "But first, I want to touch those luscious tits."

Once he'd unbuttoned her blouse, Matt shoved it off her shoulders. As the warmth it held in dissipated, her nipples puckered even tighter against the satiny fabric of her bra and tingled with need.

He reached around behind her and deftly unhooked her bra. Pulling it off, he tossed it across the room. "Oh, yes," he growled, then leaned down to engulf one stiff pink nipple in his mouth.

Her nipples had always been so very sensitive, but this was nirvana. He alternately sucked and released, adding flicks of his tongue over the taut nub. She shuddered as he switched over to her other breast, his hand caressing the one he'd left behind. The sensations from his ministrations on both nipples weakened her ability to form clear thoughts. Thoughts other than how Matt was toying with her body.

But she wanted more. She wanted to take pleasure in giving the same back to him. "My turn," she declared.

She gave him a gentle shove toward the bed. By the time they both got there, all their clothes were scattered over the hardwood floor.

Dear heavens, he's so damned hot. She stroked his broad shoulders and hard pecs, then down the trail of crisp hair heading right toward his thick cock. Catching his gaze, she slowly licked her lips.

Once she was certain he knew what she was about to do, she settled beside his hips. With feather light caresses, she stroked up and down his shaft and over his balls.

She leaned down and engulfed the tip of his cock with her lips. Matt raked his fingers through his hair then fisted his hands in the pillow, groaning. She wanted to take him so close to the edge, he'd have to struggle to keep control.

She licked and sucked, teasing him with depth and then just barely touching him with the tip of her tongue. As his hips rose up to meet her, Suz knew her goal was in sight. She'd always relished doing this with lovers for it gave her a pure rush of female power. But this, with Matt, was a whole new level of wonderful.

"Dear gawd, woman ... I can't hold back much longer." Matt's words came out ragged, his voice thick with need.

"What is it you want, Matthew?"

"Ride me."

His simple request was all the encouragement she needed. She let his cock slip from her mouth after giving it a final lick and kiss. With that, she repositioned herself, sitting up on her heels.

"Hand me that packet."

Matt slid one hand under the other pillow and pulled out the wrapped condom they'd tucked under there earlier. "Want me to—?"

She shook her head. "It's my turn, mister. Hand it over," she said, holding out her hand.

Once she'd positioned the latex sheath at the tip of his cock, she pushed it down, gripping his erection in her fist and changing pressure with each finger. Tormenting him.

He gritted his teeth and fisted the pillow again. "You keep this up and I'm not going to last more than a few strokes."

"I'm betting you can." Swinging one leg over his hips, she lowered herself until she barely touched his cock. "Tell me again, Matt. Tell me what you want me to do."

He gripped her hips. "Ride me," he ordered, pulling her down onto him. "Ride me hard."

With that, Suz begin to drive her hips, slow and sensual, in a circle on his axis, first one direction and then the other. She was so close to the edge... He held her hips, while she gripped his forearms for balance. Stopping those slow circles, changing her rhythm, she began moving up and down.

"Harder," she moaned, relishing how well he filled her.

"Not...gonna...last," Matt groaned.

"Me neither."

Their rhythm grew faster, more frantic.
When she felt her control begin to slip, Suz
gripped his arms harder. "Now, Matt.
Please"

Beneath her, he arched up, driving as deep as possible, and he trembled as his climax swept through him. Her inner spasms gripped his shaft, the pressure building until she exploded into a thousand stars.

As the spasms melted into tiny quivers, she fell forward onto his chest with her face against his shoulder. She struggled, but finally got her breathing slowed from ragged gasps.

"That was..."

"Yeah, it was," Matt sighed.

Seconds ticked by as she listened to his breathing and heartbeat. "We should, umm, tidy up."

He nodded. "I'll get rid of this." His fingers slid between them to hold the condom as he slid free from her body.

Once they'd both taken turns in the bathroom and returned to his bed, she once again snuggled against his shoulder. "This is going to be one of the benefits of having to stay here for a while."

"I'm glad you think so." He kissed the top of her head and hugged her closer.

"Do you believe I'm really in danger?" She draped her arm over him, returning the hug.

He didn't answer right away, obviously thinking about his words. "I'm not sure whether or not it was a case of mistaken identity. You were wearing one of Marianne's dresses. You had your back to where the shooter was hiding. The two of you are similar enough in build. You could possibly be confused with my cousin."

She'd been so focused on her nightmares, Suz hadn't really considered that angle. She and Marianne had been swapping clothes since their college days. "She has been taking the brunt of the threats."

"That's why we've been so overprotective with her. It drives Gray crazy when she goes someplace she didn't tell him about in advance."

Suz cringed inside, remembering the day about a month ago when she and Marianne had dashed over to Louisville for a bit of retail therapy. Gray had caught up with them, storming into the lingerie section, threatening to drag her to the car if necessary.

"I get it. I just hope this all gets sorted out. The sooner the better."

"You and me both, hun." He stroked his hand down her arm. "You and me both."

Chapter 10

"Jess, we need to talk." Terri walked into Detective Kent's office, closing the door behind her.

"This looks serious." Jessica Kent closed the folder she'd been reviewing.

"The rifle from the MacInnes incident. We got a partial."

The detective sat straight up in her chair. "I.D.?"

"Nothing conclusive."

"Why do I hear a big, fat *but* in your voice?"

"'Cause you do." Terri handed over a sheet of paper. "The weapon's been wiped. By someone who knew what they were doing."

"Like a cop?"

The ballistics tech nodded. "Could be. But that always makes me look in the nooks and crannies. First off, there are marks on the finish consistent with optics mounting. When the gun was taken into custody, there were no optics in place."

"And Matt MacInnes said in his statement it was a lens flare that alerted him." Jess's suspicions tingled in anticipation. "About that partial?"

"I was getting to that. I actually found a couple. One matches Officer Mendez who is documented as having cleared the weapon when it was logged into custody. And here's where it gets dicey." She scooted her chair closer to the desk. "The other partial," her voice dropped to a bare whisper. "I found it on the magazine. It pinged to Sheriff Whitaker."

"Oh, shit."

# # #

Suz ran into Gray heading down the hall toward the conference room next to Colin's office. "Got the buffet menu ready?"

With a wicked gleam in his eyes, the distillery chef nodded. "Oh yeah, you're gonna love it."

As they opened the conference room door, they could hear Colin already talking to someone. "Yes, I'll pass that information on, detective. And again, thank you for keeping us informed."

Suz and Gray settled into empty chairs around the table. "Detective Kent?" Gray asked.

Colin nodded. "She let me know that they can now tie the rifle from the shooting to Sheriff Whitaker."

"You mean the one that almost shot me was the county sheriff?"

"'Fraid so. At least there's evidence to support that theory." He flipped open a file folder. "She also wanted to caution me."

"About what?" Gray asked.

"The holiday party. She suggested we spring for some extra security."

Suz remembered the last conversation they'd had with the detective. "She's afraid the brains behind all of this is still out there."

"That might not be a bad idea, Col. Can the distillery afford it?" Gray voiced the question that had also popped into Suz's mind.

"I'll talk that over with Dad. She said she'd give us names of some off duty and trustworthy officers. They might be willing to earn some extra off-duty money."

"They'd be spread pretty damned thin. We'd need a few at the event center and some stationed at various parts around the grounds." Gray stared off in the distance for a moment, obviously thinking about an alternative. "Too bad we couldn't get Colonel Beckley and his reservists."

Colin smiled at his friend. "Might be worth a phone call. They've done a couple of deployments. Might be worth considering. Couldn't do it on Uncle Sugar's weekend though."

"Would have to be on their own time for sure."

"Yeah, I'll keep everyone in the loop on what Dad and I decide. Now, where are we on the food?"

Gray laid out his menu. "I'll be setting it up in a buffet format. And I've worked out a rotation for the kitchen staff so that no one has to miss the entire party. There will no passed apps. And Suz has arranged for two paid bartenders."

"Contracts are all signed for them and the DJ. I've already met with your employee volunteers for decorating that afternoon."

"Either of you have any problems or concerns?" Colin asked.

"I'm good." Gray said.

"Me, too." Suz said, then added, "Gray sent me the dimensions of the buffet table he needed."

"Okay. Two weeks till party time. All distillery employees, a few city and KDA folks. Plus a handful of contractors we work with during the year. A just us chickens party to round out the year."

Chairs scooted away from the table as they all stood.

"I need to get back to the kitchen," Gray said, waving goodbye.

"Got a minute, Suz?" Colin asked.

"Sure. What's up?"

He rubbed his fingers over the side of his face. "You doing okay?"

"Yeah." She nodded. "Matt will hardly let me out of his sight. He went with me to the party supply store yesterday evening after work. The man was bored stiff."

"I can imagine. I went with Jenni once." He shook his head. "Never again. Do I need to walk you over to the cooperage?"

"I don't think so. It won't even take me five minutes." She shoved her notebook into the oversized bag she used both as a purse and work supply storage. Hefting it right in front of Colin, she added, "I swing this at anyone, they're going down."

"I have no doubt." As they both headed to the door, he said, "Remind Matt, if he hasn't already done it, to make sure he's gotten his hunting license and deer tags. We're going muzzle loader season this year."

They walked down the hall toward the stairs. "Trust me, he's more than ready. My dad never did any hunting, so this is all new to me."

Colin laughed. "Then you're in for a treat. Mom makes a killer venison stew. Dad and Uncle Wes hide out in the garage making sausage the next day after their hunt. Makes for a great weekend breakfast."

"I'll have to take your word for it, for now at least. I'm game to try most anything."

As she turned to go down the stairs, Colin grabbed her arm. "Be careful. Being with you is making my cousin happy. He got his heart broken pretty bad about ten years ago and hasn't been this serious about anyone since."

"He never mentioned—"

"And neither did I." He put a finger to his lips.

"Ah, okay." She promised herself to find out more about that, soon.

He gave her a quick kiss on the cheek before she bounded down the stairs to the first floor. Once outside, she headed straight over to the cooperage.

Matt had already locked up and had the VW running. "How'd you know?"

"Col texted."

"Figures." She put her purse in the back before settling in the passenger's seat and buckled the seat belt.

As Matt headed down the drive, toward the road, Suz wondered if she should somehow broach the subject of Matt's heartbreak. *Better not, at least not now.*

# # #

Madelyn Barnes sorted through the stack of mail she'd been avoiding for over a week. "What's this?"

The large, squarish envelope had the logo and return address from the MacInnes Distillery. She slit the flap open and removed the card inside. As she read the embossed script, she broke out in a smile which immediately became laughter over the irony of it all.

Those thieving MacInneses had the audacity to invite her to their annual holiday gathering. She'd heard about their annual gathering, of course. They'd started back in her grandfather's day. Employees. KDA leaders. Contractors. And people like her. People who made things happen.

The perfect opportunity to exact revenge—to bring them down. Now she had a legitimate reason to be at the distillery and carry out the plan that had started to form in her mind.

Fire. Beautiful. Cleansing. Deadly.

She'd seen more than one distillery fire in her life. They burned hot, so hot. All that alcohol and wood would go up like an old-fashioned roman candle.

And it spread, rick to rick, warehouse to warehouse. Destroying everything in its searing path, causing millions of dollars in damage.

That's what she wanted. *Needed.* To put an end to the MacInnes empire—one built on her family's recipe. It should have been her. Her name, her money.

She'd go to their party, eat their food, drink their bourbon. Then she'd start the chaos.

# # #

Matt tapped the hoop into place, inching it down on the barrel, glad for the time alone with his work and his thoughts.

Suz.

He couldn't get her out of his mind. How she refused to wear shoes without socks. How she took her coffee. And how scared she was when a nightmare startled her awake in the middle of the night.

He was hooked. In less than two months, he was caught hook, line, and sinker. Funny how none of that scared him. It always had in the past. He'd felt himself maybe falling for some girl. Didn't matter where or how, but he'd bail. He'd let them down as easily as he could, but he'd end it. Now, he knew why.

"Hey, got a minute?"

"Sure, but come here. Tell me if this looks level."

Suz walked up and gave him one of those you've-got-to-be-kidding looks. "You're the master cooper and you're asking me if that hoop is level?"

"So sue me." He shrugged and put down the tools. "That might be an excuse to do this."

He pulled her into the workshop and slid the door shut before pushing her up against the wooden wall. Gripping both of her wrists in one of his hands, he pressed them against the wall over her head.

Then, he captured her lips with his, kissing her hard and deep as he wedged his knee between hers, her.slim skirt stopping his progress.

"Damn, you've got your grown-up clothes on."

Her lips curled up in a smile against his. "Yeah, I need to run over to Lexington for a meeting."

His gut tightened into a knot. "Can't you do it on Zoom or something?"

"As much as I wish I could," she shook her head, "I've got to see this venue first hand."

He pulled away from her. "Give me a few minutes to close things up around here."

"You can do that? Just close things up to go with me?"

"Today, yes. Once in a while, no. But, today, you're in luck." He hung his tools up on the wall and then checked to make sure that the charring flame had gone out. "By the way, cheese-burgers are on you when you get finished with your meeting."

"You're on." She gave his ass a playful smack.

# # #

"I can't get the idea out of my head that something's going to happen soon," Marianne said to the ladies.

The four of them, Marianne, Jenni, Charlotte, along with Suz had driven over to Louisville, with the excuse of getting holiday shopping started. They actually had done some—mostly for the guys. Then Jenni spotted a frozen custard place across the parking lot, and they all agreed it was time for a break.

"I get it," Suz added. "I've been seeing shadows where there aren't any." She scooped up a spoonful then licked the spoon off.

"If any of you mention this to Gray, I will deny it to my dying day." Marianne pointed a finger around the table. "I threw a pillow at Colonel Taylor the other night when he pushed the bedroom door open."

The mental image of her friend sitting up in bed throwing a pillow at the cat had them all fighting back giggles. "At least you didn't wake Gray," Suz said. "You're right he'd never let you live it down. At least in private."

Charlotte swirled her straw through her milkshake before looking over at Suz. "Any news about the shooting?"

"Damn, we didn't tell you."

With Jenni and Marianne chiming in here and there, Suz shared the evidence linking Sheriff Whitaker to the gun and then the ballistic information regarding the bullet recovered at the distillery. "It's enough to convince me."

Jenni nodded in agreement. "Colin and I, too."

"Yeah," Marianne added. "But get this, Detective Kent thinks he wasn't acting alone. That someone was pulling his strings, at least on this."

Charlotte pulled a small notepad and pen out of her purse, then hastily scribbled down a note. "You know, that makes sense in a weird sort of way."

"Doesn't it?" Suz added.

"Have you told her yet," Marianne gently elbowed Suz in the ribs.

"About?" Suz tried to look confused and yet feared she knew exactly what her friend was referring to.

"Your nightmares, goofball. You know what I mean."

Does everyone have to know? "I, umm, I think."

Charlotte, bless her, must've figured out Suz didn't want to talk about the nightmares. "You and I." The journalist reached over to give Suz's hand a squeeze. "We I can talk about them later and you let me know if you even want me to put that in the story at all."

Suz gave the other woman a smile of thanks. "It's going to be uncomfortable, but I think it would need to go in, at least some." She turned so she partially faced all three of the women. "I, well, I'm starting to talk with a therapist. Matt suggested I find someone. I'm not sure I'm making any progress, but at least I haven't had any more nightmares." Suz paused for a moment. "At least not after that last horrible one."

She gave them a very glossed over account of the dreams, including the last one. "I'm learning that the dreams are my subconscious trying to understand and take control over a situation I had no control over."

"I bet, too, you're glad you've got Matt around." Jenni pointed with her sundae spoon.

"Actually, yeah, I am." She scraped her spoon on the bottom of the paper cup. "And ya know what, ladies? I think I might be falling for him."

# # #

"Hurry up, Matt. I need to get over to the event center before the party."

He headed down the stairs as he cinched and fastened his belt. "Do I really have to wear a jacket?"

She rolled her eyes at him as he made the corner of the landing and then down the final three steps. "Yes, both Colin and Gray are. Come here, let me straighten that tie."

Once she had him looking what she obviously considered appropriate, Suz stepped back and gave him the once over. "Oh yes, you'll do."

"You'll more than do. I love that dress, but don't you think it's a bit..."

She crossed her arms over her bared cleavage. "A bit what?"

He fought down his jealousy. The soft knit fabric clung to each and every curve. But what the exposed curves of her breasts did to him, he supposed would do to other men at the party. "A bit too revealing. You're showing an awful lot of these." Matt trailed a finger over her rounded breasts.

"Nothing more than I have many times in the past." She paused a moment, looking right into his eyes. "Oh, I see. Someone might be a wee bit possessive?" She followed the comment with a flirty wink.

"Maybe." He drew the single word response out into multiple syllables. "A little bit."

Matt debated dipping into his pocket and retrieving the present he'd gotten her to go along with his question about being exclusive. But with her being in that much of a hurry, he figured he'd wait until they got back home after the party. Maybe until tomorrow, since nothing would change between now and the morning.

She went up on her tiptoes to give him a quick kiss. "Come on, handsome. Let's go party."

# # #

Judge Barnes shoved the folded walker onto the back seat of her car. *The ruse has to be maintained.* Just like at the campaign dinner. She grinned to herself. No one had even breathed a whisper of suspicion surrounding the untimely death of Sheriff Whitaker. No, she'd gotten away with it once more.

She already had the wrapped packet of flares sitting in the front seat. Since the night Whitaker had brought them to her, she'd looked them over carefully until she was certain she could set them off in a hurry. The only challenge was going to be disappearing from the party long enough to carry out her plan.

How very thoughtful of that thieving MacInnes clan to have built their new event center at the top of the hill, at the head of the row where their oldest barrel warehouses currently stood. *I'm sure they thought it photogenic. A nod to their history even.* A history that should, by rights, belong to the Barnes family. *To me.*

Madelyn remembered clearly the day of the ribbon cutting when the six new rickhouses had been completed. She'd been a successful lawyer in her thirties, contemplating her first run at the bench. Still a very little fish in a massive pond, she'd vowed then and there to someday, somehow, exact revenge for what they'd done to her father and grandfather. And that day was finally at hand.

This will be the distillery fire of the century.

# # #

Suz made her final walk around the party room before officially opening the doors. The caterer had a fabulous buffet table set out. Gray had hovered like a mother hen when that staff had invaded his kitchen space to finish the final prep of the appetizers and small plate offerings. The D.J. was nearly finished with his own set up after she'd reminded him to mix holiday music with a danceable selection in addition to a few country music classics.

Coatroom? Check. Party bars stocked and staffed? Check. Door prizes? Check.

She tamped down her nerves and pulled in a deep breath. This was her first event as an almost part of the family. She couldn't let Matt and the rest of the MacInnesses down. *This better be a success.*

Nodding over to Jim and Wes MacInnes so they could throw open the big double doors, she borrowed the DJ's mic and announced, "Okay everyone. It's time to party!"

The first hour went by in a blur. Suz flitted around the room, being more the event planner than Matt's date. *Stop it.* Once she'd realized what she was doing, she forced herself to let go of the reins. She'd chosen a fabulous caterer in Jacob's company. *Step back and let him do his job.* Same with the DJ and the clean-up crew.

She searched the faces in the crowd. There, talking with Colin, Detective Kent, and a man Suz hadn't seen before was Matt. She was his date after all. *Time to start acting like it.*

Sliding up beside him and threading her fingers between his, she stood silent for a moment, catching up with the conversation in progress. Matt gave her fingers a squeeze as she listened.

"We don't have a solid suspect in Whitaker's murder. Hell, we barely have a person of interest," Kent said. "And that one possibility, well, it's almost unthinkable."

"Dr. Graham, I don't believe you've met my date,." Matt broke the short silence. "Suz, this is Jess's friend James Graham, Franklin County's medical examiner. Jim, Suz Benton, event planner extraordinaire."

"Nice to meet you Dr. Graham." Suz offered her hand, and he took it.

"Please, it's Jim. Or at least James. I get way too much Dr. Graham at work."

She smiled. "Oh, I like James. It suits you somehow."

The warmth of his smile intensified. "My mom thought so, as the alternative was going to be Edwin after my grandfather."

"No offence to your grandfather, but you got the best of that deal."

James chuckled. "I completely agree."

"Back to the suspect conversation." Matt changed the topic. "You're certain Whitaker was murdered?"

Jess nodded. "Guaranteed. I can't really talk about the details, you understand. But with what Jim found on autopsy, it's a solid case for murder."

"I admit," Suz added, "I'm a murder mystery junkie. Dad got me hooked with old Quincy reruns when I was in middle school."

"Okay, that's enough murder talk." Matt gave Suz's hand a tug. "I'm taking my date out onto the dance floor."

Before they turned around. James reached out to Jess. "We can't let them have all the fun, now can we?"

# # #

Madelyn sipped her lightly spiked eggnog, watching the crowd. Little groups scattered around the room, laughing and conversing. Some gathered over by the buffet table in a passionate discussion, obviously the foodies of the crowd, probably playing armchair chef. And a handful of brave couples were slow-dancing to the Christmas music.

Even that blasted girl Whitaker mistook for Marianne and the useless cousin. As another couple followed them, Madelyn couldn't resist a smile. *Detective Kent.* And oh my, if it wasn't the medical examiner, Dr Graham.

Look how they have everyone fooled. Anger roiled up inside her. *Doesn't anyone else see these MacInnesses as the thieves they are?* She looked around the festive party room, all decked out in the greens and reds of the holiday season. *Ah yes, there they are, Jim and Wes, the current patriarchs of the family. Clueless, riding on the coattails of the Barnes mash bill. We'll soon see what happens when it all goes up in flames.*

"Good afternoon, Judge Barnes. I hope you're enjoying the party."

Madelyn looked up to find the one MacInnes, above all of the others, she could not abide. Marianne, the one slated to follow in her uncle's footsteps as master distiller. Madelyn pasted on her best fake smile. "It's a lovely party, Ms. MacInnes. Thank you for the invitation. I realize I'm no longer one of the movers and shakers of the Commonwealth."

Marianne shook her head. "Nonsense, Judge. Personally, I love to celebrate powerful women at all phases of their careers. Why, look what your endorsement did for Sheriff Whitaker the past two elections." Her face clouded over. "I'm so sorry. I shouldn't have mentioned him. I know the two of you were good friends, in addition to being political allies."

"It's all right. At my age, you lose friends almost daily."

The younger woman's smile warmed back up a bit. "Again, thanks for coming, Judge."

Judge Barnes watched Marianne walk away. *Trollop. All but living with that man.* Right in front of her parents, too. *Why, in my day…*

Focus. She began to slowly head toward the doors. *It's showtime.*

Chapter 11

It began as a murmur in one corner of the room, over by the tall narrow windows. Spreading rapidly through the crowd, it snowballed as it went.

Fire!

"Everyone, please, stay calm!" Colin urged the crowd. "As a precaution for your safety, if you would, please, gather your important belongings. Catering staff, please follow Gray out through the kitchen.

"Guests, you may exit out the doors to the patio. From there, you'll be directed toward the brick admin building, where you will be warm and safe. Do not, I repeat, *do not* make a dash for your vehicle. The fire department is on its way and we don't want to slow them down by clogging up the road from town."

After giving Suz a quick kiss and eliciting a promise to get out of the building as soon as possible, Matt rushed outside to his assigned spot, manning a hose to protect the second and third rickhouse in the row from the one already burning.

That one, he knew, was already a loss, considering how rapidly the flames consumed the aged wood of both the building and the barrels. And with all that bourbon literally adding fuel to the flames, they'd be lucky if the fire was confined to this one rickhouse.

His heart ached for those barrels. His cousin Marianne would moan the loss of the bourbon inside. But barrels were a reflection of the cooper's art and skill, held together with nothing more than pressure from the iron hoops and the swollen wood—along with the cooper's talent in choosing just the right arrangement of the curved oaken staves. That cut him to the core.

The first rickhouse, now completely engulfed in flames, burned higher and so much hotter. So hot in fact, it threatened to push Matt and his water hose away. But he'd survived the heat of the middle eastern desert summer with a full Marine Corps patrol pack.

Hold on, hold on. In the distance, the first wail of the sirens split the night. *Don't let those flames jump the gap between the buildings.*

# # #

Marianne and Suz were being tasked with getting all the elderly guests out of the building. There was no mistaking the red and orange flames outside the windows now.

And the guests still inside were beginning to panic. Worried about walking up the drive to the admin building, about the safety of their vehicles, and not to mention the cold December evening.

Finally, they'd gotten every guest out the door and up the walk, assisted by other distillery staff. "Let's switch the lights off and get the hell outta dodge."

Marianne popped out of the swinging door to the kitchen. "I got the lights in there."

"Stop right there. Both of you."

# # #

"Judge Barnes." Both Suz and Marianne gasped.

"Well, well, well. If it isn't the MacInnes bitch and her sidekick." Madelyn couldn't believe her luck. Not only was the warehouse gloriously aflame, but now she had the chance to finish the job that fool Whitaker had fumbled. She let her hand slide into the bag slung on her shoulder, fingers gripping the revolver.

"Two birds with one stone, so to speak."

"We were just about to leave," Sidekick said as she tried to inch backward.

The MacInnes bitch added, "Yes, Judge. Let's get out of here. As a safety precaution."

The bitch tried to grip Madelyn by the elbow. "Get your hand off me, you thieving MacInnes."

"What did you just call me?"

"You heard me." Madelyn pulled the revolver from her bag. "Get over there with your prissy friend," she motioned with the gun. "You and all the others in the MacInnes family. Thieves, the lot of you."

Marianne stood next to her friend. "Wh...What do you think we stole?"

"I don't think. I know."

Madelyn struggled to keep her hand steady as anger boiled inside her chest. They weren't any different from all the thieves she'd sentenced through her years on the bench. "My grandfather's recipe, that's what."

"Recipe? What recip—" The confusion cleared from the other woman's face. "Our mash bill? Elmer's mash bill?"

"See, you even admit it." Madelyn brought the pistol up. "It belonged to my grandfather. Now it belongs to me. All of this belongs to me."

"No, Judge Barnes, it doesn't." Marianne shook her head. "My family paid damn good money for that mash bill."

Madelyn gritted her teeth, seething inside. "No. My father told me all about it. How he was forced to sell."

"I'm afraid your father wasn't quite truthful with you, Judge."

"I knew you'd deny it." Madelyn gripped her wrist to steady the gun.

"Your grandfather, Elmer, was one of the best master distillers. It was his mash bill that enabled MacInnes to be approved for continued operation during prohibition. But your father, between bad investments and his gambling—"

"Stop right there. My father was no gambler." She fought the shaking as she put her thumb up on the hammer.

"I'm sure he tried to hide it from you, Judge. Any father would." Marianne's voice quivered.

"But, but..."

"MacInnes bought the rights fair and square. I...I can show you the papers, if you'll put the gun down."

"It can't be. No, it can't. Daddy would never have sold the recipe." Her grip tightened on her weapon.

"I'm so sorry to be the one to tell you the truth. But yes, he did."

"No. No. No."

Madelyn dragged in a deep breath as she pulled the hammer back and squeezed the trigger.

# # #

The sirens got closer and closer as Matt tried desperately to hold his position between two warehouses. Wooden ricks full of bourbon-filled barrels burned so fast, he was being repeatedly pushed back by the intense heat. Out of nowhere, just as the first fire engine rolled up, above the roar of the fire came one gunshot. And a second right on its heels.

Then, over everything else, a scream that tore straight to his heart. "Suz!" Matt dropped the hose and ran toward the event center. "Not again."

His pulse raced as he ran as fast as he could, his fear soaring with each stride. *Please, please, don't let it be her.*

He dashed up the concrete walk before tearing open the double doors. "Suz? Suz? You okay?"

His gaze darted around the room, then shock registered at what he saw. There, on the dance floor, in a crumpled heap lay Judge Barnes, a growing crimson stain in the middle of her chest. "What happened?" He knelt on one knee beside her body to check for a pulse.

"Is she...?" Marianne's voice trembled with the question.

Matt nodded. "'Fraid so," he added as he stood back up. "Looks like she had a gun, but why did you shoot her?"

"Sh...she didn't," Suz said. "I did."

Before any of them could say another word, Colin, Gray and a handful of other distillery employees stormed through the doors. "What happened?" Colin demanded.

"I shot Judge Barnes," Suz murmured.

"Stop. Don't say another word." Jess Kent walked in past the knot of men from the distillery. She, too, knelt to check for the judge's pulse. "Okay folks, this is now my scene. Jim, get your team here. Colin, you've got a fire on your hands. Go. But if the distillery's lawyer is here tonight, send him or her over."

# # #

"And then what?" Detective Kent asked.

Suz looked at the other woman across the table. "I heard her cock back the hammer. She was going to shoot Marianne," she declared.

"So, where did you get the gun?" Jess scribbled down a note.

Suz took another drink from her glass of water, trying once again to settled her nerves. "Back in the summer, when she was the focus of the attacks, Marianne started carrying. The judge was so focused on her, I got her gun out. Matt's been teaching me to shoot."

"Oh? And were those lessons your idea?" Jess asked.

"Stop it right there." Marianne smacked her hands down on the table.

"May I remind you, you are sitting here as a courtesy, Marianne? Only because this is *not* a formal interview." Jess closed the notebook. "If I thought even for a moment that either of you did this on purpose—"

"Okay, okay." Marianne leaned back in her seat.

"We're done for today." Jess stood and pushed the chair back under the table. "I want both of you in my office first thing in the morning. I'm already breaking protocol by not separating you two."

"Hey, lieutenant?"

"Yah, Mike?"

"Found the bullet." The crime scene tech held up a clear plastic bag. "We also got the judge's revolver and the one Ms. Benton used."

"If the evidence matches the story, that one should be a match for Judge Barnes' weapon. We'll see which gun the bullet from the judge's body matches which gun, too."

Suz rose to her feet. "Can I go home now?"

# # #

The mantle clock chimed three o'clock in the middle of the night when Suz hung up her jacket, and kicked off her high heels. She leaned back against the sofa arm, rubbing first one foot and then the other. "Ahh, but it feels good to get those shoes off."

"I can imagine." Matt clicked the dead bolt closed on the front door. "Though on behalf of myself, and all of the other men in the world, you looked damn good in them this evening."

She wrapped her arms around his neck. "Like how I look in this new dress, huh?"

Matt hugged her close, his hands cupping her backside. "Like isn't actually the word, gorgeous. And I don't even mind other guys admiring the view." He gave her a squeeze. "I know who gets to take you home."

"Yes, you do. Which, by the way, I'm ready to head to bed. And before you say anything," she placed a finger on his lips, "I plan on going to sleep."

"Me, too. Snuggled up against my girl." He moved one hand and delved into one of his suit coat pockets. "There's just one piece of business before we go to bed."

"What's this?" she asked when he handed her a box from one of the local jewelers.

"I want to make something clear between us. We're exclusive. Right?"

"Please tell me you don't have any sort of question about this, Matt." She opened the box. Nestled in the cotton fluff lay a silver chain. She lifted it up and dangling from the chain was a small silver barrel. "It's lovely."

She lifted her hair then handed the necklace to him. "Put it on me."

He muttered a curse under his breath, obviously struggling with the clasp. Finally, he got it fastened and let the barrel settle against her skin, right at the top of her cleavage. "Let's go to bed now."

# # #

"What smells so good?" Jim Graham wrapped one arm around Jess's waist and began nibbling her neck. "I'm starving."

"Nothing fancy, just shepherd's pie. My Irish granny's recipe." Jess turned in his embrace, kissing him long and deep. "You've got about fifteen, maybe twenty, minutes. I need to get it out of the oven and let it sit for a bit before we eat."

"Granny must've been a damned fine cook."

"She was." Jess took the baking dish from the oven and set it on one of the empty burners to cool.

"That'll give me enough time to grab a quick shower. I've been in court all afternoon around those lawyers." He faked a shudder. "I feel so dirty." With a wink, he headed upstairs.

Half an hour later, they were enjoying dinner, talking over their days. "Remember the Wendel Cleary shooting back last spring?" Jess asked.

Jim thought for a few moments before nodding. "That first break in at the MacInnes Distillery?"

She nodded. "One and the same." Jess took a bite of the brown gravy laden mashed potatoes and swallowed before continuing. "The bullet you took from him was a match for one of those from last week's shooting at the distillery."

"Let me guess. The one from Judge Barnes' revolver." He used a chunk of biscuit to push the last of the veggies onto his fork.

"Give the man a gold star. And you know what? It's looking like Madelyn Barnes was the mastermind behind this whole thing. When we searched the house, we found a burner phone and copious notes. We had the burner traced. She'd even warned Pettijohn to lay low."

"She really had it bad to ruin the distillery."

"Sure seems like it. My team is still looking through all the stuff we recovered at her home." She gathered up their plates. "We also found dried foxglove stored in a bottle like you would herbs and spices."

"You think she's the one who poisoned Sheriff Whitaker?" Jim followed her with the casserole dish.

"Might never be able to prove it, but my gut says yes." Opening the dishwasher door, she started loading in the plates and silverware. "I figure he was the last thread leading back to her. A woman like her would want all the loose ends dealt with."

"Definitely."

Something's not right with Jim tonight. He'd been looking around and his conversation lacked his usual lightheartedness. *That's it. Enough.*

"What's wrong?" Jess demanded.

"Wrong? Nothing's wrong."

"Please. How long have I known you? If nothing's wrong, then you're rolling something 'round and 'round in that scientific brain of yours. Puzzling case at work?" She took the leftover apple pie from two nights ago out of the fridge. "Big piece or little one?"

He gripped her wrist, stopping her. "Stop for a moment."

Her hand started shaking. "What's wrong?"

"Nothing. I simply want to ask you something important."

"So, ask."

"Move in with me? Or marry me if you'd prefer. I'm tired of this crazy bouncing back and forth between my place and yours. Or we can find something together. Just pick one. Please."

She dropped the pie server onto the counter. "I... I thought you, umm, never wanted to marry again," she said, swallowing hard.

"When Georgia and I split up, I wanted nothing to do with it. But now," he shrugged. "Now, well, I think we're right for one another."

Did she dare? "Yes."

"Which?" His face went from relieved to confused in a split second.

"Eh, we'll figure it out as we go."

# # #

Matt's mom pulled Suz into a big hug as she walked through the great room at Marianne's parents' house. Suz returned Gloria's embrace, while at the same time trying not to drop the dried apple stack cake.

"Kitchen?" Suz asked.

Gloria pointed across the room to the open concept kitchen. "Over there." She lifted the aluminum foil covering. "That looks delicious. My mother used to make those for the holidays, too."

"Mine, too."

Gloria hugged her son. "Matthew, take the girl's coat and put it in Colin's old room. But be careful with the dessert."

Matt rolled his eyes. "Yes, Mom. I think I can handle that."

"Here, take my purse." Then Suz let him help her with her coat while balancing the cake first in one hand, then the other.

"Oh, this is lovely." Gloria very lightly touched the silver barrel resting against Suz's sweater.

"Matt picked it out." She debated adding that she and Matt had upped the ante on their relationship.

"He told me he was going to get you something special. Looks like he made a good choice." Gloria gave her a smile that spoke volumes. "With the woman, too."

"Matt told you?"

"He said there wasn't anything official, but that the two of you were, how did he put it, exclusive."

Suz nodded. "Neither of us will be seeing anyone else."

Gloria squeezed her. "You're coming over tomorrow, right?"

"Of course. Cookies are baked and the sweet potato casserole is in the fridge, ready to bake tomorrow morning."

They joined the rest of the family in the den, finding a heated game of euchre in progress. Marianne and Wes were partnered against Gray and Marianne's dad, Jim. The lead went back and forth a few times but in the end, Marianne took the final trick pushing their score to ten.

"I demand a rematch," Gray announced as he scooped up the cars to begin another round.

"Deal 'em, slick. I'm feeling especially lucky this evening." Marianne interlaced her fingers, flipped her wrists, and stretched her arms out over the table like some nineteenth century riverboat gambler.

"Oh, really? Care to make a wager on that?" Gray shuffled the cards.

Suz nudged her friend in the ribs. "Go for it, girl."

"Best two outta three. Winner gets a back rub from the loser."

"I win either way." Gray offered her the opportunity to cut, which Marianne declined.

Jim made a show of covering his ears. "There are certain things a father doesn't want to think about."

Matt got up and left the room, returning in a few moments. "Hey, while you're in between games, Dad, Uncle Jim. I found this picture in one of the albums stored in the attic at Aunt Muriel's. I gotta show it to you."

"What picture?" Matt's father, Wes, asked.

Shrugging, Matt handed the old photo to his father. "That's what we want to know. It's wasn't mounted in the album, just tucked inside the front cover. We know it's you and Uncle Jim." He touched the picture. "But who's the girl? Some cousin we've never met?"

Wes's face froze as he looked down at the photo. His hands started to shake as he handed it over to his brother. "Jim, you need to take a look at this."

Jim, Colin and Marianne's dad, took the picture. His eyes went wide. "Uh huh. You found this at Aunt Muriel's?"

"Yeah, Uncle Jim. It was in a photo album, pushed between the pages, in one of her trunks."

Jim MacInnes stared at the picture and slowly shook his head. He scrubbed one hand over his chin and lips before saying anything. Finally, he inhaled deep. "I figured that would come back to bite us in the ass."

"Yes, we know who she is." Pause. "That's Katie. Katie MacInnes." He visibly steeled himself. "Our older sister. Your aunt."

Matt's grip tightened on Suz's hand. "Aunt? What happened? Did she, uh, die or something?"

Wes shook his head and shrugged. "We don't know."

"What the hell do you mean, you don't know?" Colin demanded. "She is, or was, your big sister. Didn't Grandpa do something?"

"Sit down, son. There's more to the story," Jim explained.

"Better be good," Colin muttered.

Jim glared over at his son. "Stow that attitude until you hear what I've got to say." He took a drink from his coffee before he started talking.

"It was just a couple of days after her high school graduation. Wes and I were still in junior high. We came in that afternoon and there was a county sheriff's car in the driveway. Katie had left the house that morning as usual for her job at the horse barn. One of the other kids had given her a ride.

"The stable manager said she'd come in like always, but just up and quit. No one has seen her since."

Suz wrapped her arm around Matt at the news that his aunt had disappeared. "An eighteen year old young woman just doesn't disappear into thin air." Matt's voice took on a cold, dangerous tone.

"Mama searched Katie's room. Her new suitcase and most of her clothes were gone, along with all the money she'd gotten as graduation presents."

"Runaway," Suz muttered.

Wes nodded. "The cops interviewed all of her friends from school, the ones at the barn. Even that jackass dude who'd broken up with her."

A breakup? "What did the jerk tell them?" A theory bubbled up in Suz's imagination. *I bet I know where this is heading.* "Any of them know where she went?"

"Not a one of them even knew she was planning to leave."

"Ten to one she was pregnant," Suz tossed out her theory.

"That's what we all figured." Jim confirmed. "Mama moped around and cried for weeks after. Daddy had us boys take all the pictures of her down and put them away so it wouldn't upset Mama. And he told us not to talk about Katie where Mama could hear." He picked up the photo again. "Guess it got to be habit."

"So, Katie never wrote? Or called?" Matt asked. "That was what, about thirty-five, thirty-six years ago?"

"A couple of months after she disappeared, Aunt Muriel got a phone call." Jim nodded. "It was Katie. It was just to tell us she was okay, and then she hung up. None of us have heard a word since then. It was a collect call, so we don't even know where it came from."

"You coulda told us, Dad." Colin shook his head. "Part of me wants to be really p.o.'d, you know."

"Me, too." "Yeah." Both Matt and Marianne agreed.

"After so long, I almost forgot about it." Jim nodded at his younger brother.

Several hours later, as everyone was gathering up coats and hats for the drive home, Matt stood motionless for a few moments, a rather pensive look on his face. Suz walked over to him and placed a hand on his shoulder.

"Penny for your thoughts."

"Oh, sorry. I was just wonderin' about her."

"Katie?"

Matt nodded. "She'd be about six years older than Dad. And if the assumptions are right,

we've got a cousin on the shady side of thirty-five."

"That'd be right." Colin stepped up into the conversation.

"The world's a whole different place than it was back before we were born, with lots of technology and stuff. We've got access to all sorts of databases." Matt pulled his phone from his shirt pocket. "Right here. Answers in seconds. Not days or even weeks."

"I think I see where you're heading with this, cuz," Marianne joined in while buttoning up her coat.

"Operation Find Aunt Katie is about to begin."

Chapter 12

About fifty miles to the west, in a red brick building just off of Whiskey Row in Louisville, Case put the final chair upside-down on the table just as the phone in his jacket pocket buzzed. Seeing the name on the screen, he smiled as he slid a finger over the tempered glass.

"Evening, Mom." He glanced at his watch. *Eight, Vegas time.* "You and Eli at supper?"

"We were, but we're heading back home now. I wanted to check and see how the soft opening went."

Case's heart swelled in pride. "We kept it kinda quiet, just invited some journalists and local VIP's. They all seemed to be having a good time." He walked over to the main electrical control panel and slowly began turning off switches. "I sent them all away with press kits. You and Eli taught me the right way to open a bar."

His mother laughed on the other end. "Well, I'm sure that MBA had something to do with it, son."

Flicking the last of the switches to turn out the lights in the bar, Case headed down the hall to the pair of elevators. "That MBA is just a piece of paper that says I know what the two of you taught me about running a successful club." He shoved the lattice gate open on the service elevator and stepped inside. "I'm about to head upstairs. Mom. This call might drop in the elevator shaft."

"Then I'll let you go. Take care and call me in a couple of days."

Case hit the button for the fourth floor. "Love you, Mom. My best to Eli."

He ended the call and closed the elevator door so the car started its ascent. Past the second floor that would soon become the private, members only, cigar bar, then past the third floor which housed his own office, the one his managers shared, and the room security would be using to watch all of the camera feeds and the club's locked liquor storage.

Finally, the car jerked to a halt. He shoved the gate open once again in the vast empty space of the fourth and top floor of the building. The one that would become his new home—where he would discover if there was a place for him in the MacInnes fold.

A place for Katie's son.

A place for Justin Case MacInnes.

THE END... for now

To catch up on the Bourbon Legacy series:
Bottled in Bond (a novella) www.books2read.com/u/
bMYerA[1]
Whiskey Business www.books2read.com/u/4DP5a7[2]
Tasting Notes www.books2read.com/u/b5W7d6[3]
And her non Legacy books
Knockin' on Heaven's Door (a paranormal tale)
https://books2read.com/u/mZqLER
Border Pursuit (romantic suspense) https://books2read.com/u/
b5W7d6[4]
Coming in Spring '24 JP dips her toes the world of myth and legend

You can follow JP on FaceBook
https://www.facebook.com/HoosierAnnie/

---

1. http://www.books2read.com/u/bMYerA

2. http://www.books2read.com/u/4DP5a7

3. http://www.books2read.com/u/b5W7d6

4.   https://books2read.com/u/b5W7d6%20

Don't miss out!

Visit the website below and you can sign up to receive emails whenever J. P. Bastin publishes a new book. There's no charge and no obligation.

https://books2read.com/r/B-A-SSYR-RJYQC

BOOKS2READ

Connecting independent readers to independent writers.

Did you love *Barrel Proof*? Then you should read *Border Pursuit*[5] by J. P. Bastin!

She's worked all of her life to prove herself in the male dominated military world. The world here she grew up. Her father's world.

PhD weapon systems developer Katherine Worthington has finally gotten the green light to field test her surveillance system. Yet once out in the woods, it seems every time she tries to control the test, she runs smack dab into a cammo clad wall named USMC Captain TJ Scott. Very sexy, very alpha, and completely different from her usual romantic fodder.

TJ fled the expectations of his family, ones that still push him to return and take his corner office place in the family business, finding

---

5. https://books2read.com/u/b5W7d6

6. https://books2read.com/u/b5W7d6

instead a home in his beloved Corps. To shore up his position, he's adopted a no-commitments policy when it comes to women.

The field test exercise becomes a real-world situation when Kat goes missing, forcing TJ to risk his military career in order to mount a south of the border rescue